THE
BOYHOOD
OF
GRACE JONES

Other Books by Jane Langton

THE BOYHOOD OF GRACE JONES

by Jane Langton

Pictures by Emily Arnold McCully

HARPER & ROW, PUBLISHERS
New York, Evanston, San Francisco, London

Library of Congress Catalog Card Number: 72-80364
Trade Standard Book Number: 06-023686-8
Harpercrest Standard Book Number: 06-023687-6

FIRST EDITION

For Mildred Brown,
and for Pat and Joe,
and for Betty and Virginia

Contents

Chapter 1

ITEM:
GIRL (UGH!)

On the morning of her first day in the Winslow S. DeForest Junior High School, Grace looked at herself in the mirror on the wall of the rooming house. There was a cold feathery feeling in the top of her chest. Staring at herself critically she made a mental list, as if she were an inspector and the person in the mirror were a package about to be delivered to a customer:

OUTSIDE OF PACKAGE

Item: Girl (Ugh!)—Grace Perkins Jones by name. (Check.)

Item: Date of birth—May 15, 1925. (Check.)

Item: Brown hair, short like a boy's. Good. (Check.)

Item: Middy—real blue-serge Navy middy, her own father's from 1918. Gorgeous. Beautiful. (Check.)

Item: First mate. (Hip hip hooray!) Tom by name, true to his ship in heart and soul, Trueblue Tom. (Check.)

Item: Tom's three-masted clipper ship, *The Flying Cloud*, his rolling deck on the bounding main, headed south-southwest around the Horn for California and the China trade! (Check.)

Item: Tom's captains, Nancy Blackett and John Walker, the bravest mariners and the stoutest hearts upon the seven seas. (Check! Check! Check!)

"Grace? Are you ready? Quick, quick. I'm afraid we're late."

Grace's mother was calling from downstairs. Hurriedly Grace crossed her arms and jerked at the bottom of the big blue-serge middy until it came off over her head. Rolling it up into a ball, she stuffed it into a paper bag, then patted and tugged at her rumpled school dress, which was brand-new.

"Coming," shouted Grace. Squeezing the bag under one arm, she picked up her new notebook and pencil case and charged down the stairs, leaping down them gallantly, three at a time. The whole rooming house shook.

The feathery feeling in Grace's chest was still there, colder and featherier than ever, as the Winslow S. DeForest Junior High School loomed up through the windshield of the car. It was a new brick building on the edge of town, sticking up between the woods on one side and the orderly rows of attached brick houses on the other. It was much larger than Grace's old junior high school in Ohio, because the city of Swedesville was larger than the suburb of Cleveland they had just moved away from. Grace stared at the big brick building anxiously, and thought about running away.

If she were a boy she could run away to sea. She would just wait inside the door of the school while her mother drove off, and then she would duck right out of the school again, run to the trolley stop, pay the fare to the train station with her lunch money, hop a freight, get off at Philadelphia, find her way to the Navy Yard, stow away in the hold of a ship, and come out of hiding when the ship was far out to sea. The captain would be angry of course, but Grace would take her punishment like a man, and then she would make herself so useful by swabbing the deck and polishing the brass and helping in the galley that the captain would be surprised and impressed, and sooner or later he would sign her on as one of the crew, and take her with him around the world. If she were a boy. But she was a girl (ugh). They would just laugh at her, and call her a tomboy, and send her straight home. It wasn't any use. Grace heaved a sigh and got out of the car.

Grace's mother was staring up at the new school

too. "I wonder if Mr. and Mrs. Winslow S. DeForest send their children to this school," she said.

"I don't know," said Grace.

"They're so rich, I don't suppose they send their children to the public schools, even when one of the schools is named after them," decided Mrs. Jones. "Oh, Grace, you *are* late, I'm afraid. Now, don't forget—your father and I will be here to meet you after school. We're all going over to look at the new house."

"Okay," said Grace. "When do we move in?"

"Next weekend. Thank goodness. Moving halfway across the country is so exhausting. I'll be so glad to get this family settled down again in a real house. Now, Grace, what's that bundle under your arm? It's not that horrible old—?"

"It's just my middy," mumbled Grace, hurrying up the walk.

"Grace! Don't you *dare* wear that awful thing in school!"

"It's just for *gym*," shouted Grace, breaking into a gallop.

"Grace!"

But Grace was safe inside the entrance hall of the school, with the heavy door jarring shut behind her.

She looked around. There was no one in sight. Dropping her notebook and pencil case on the floor, Grace whipped her father's middy out of its paper bag, pulled it over her head, and shook it down to

4

its full length, so that it hid everything but the hem of her new school dress from Dixie Brothers Dry Goods Store. There! Now she felt more like herself, Tom of *The Flying Cloud*, Trueblue Tom, that swashbuckling daring young sailor, fresh from a voyage around the world, ashore for the first time in a new port of call, striding along with a rolling gait, his eyes alight with curiosity, his nose quivering with new exotic scents—orange blossoms, bananas, coffee beans, monkeys and donkeys, nutty Spanish ale with the trade winds blowing.

But there were no trade winds blowing in the corridor of the Winslow S. DeForest Junior High School. There was a fragrance in the air, but even with her eyes closed Grace would have known it meant school, because it was a familiar mixture of bland steamy smells from the school cafeteria, and strong disinfectant smells from the showers, and clean waxy smells from the floor of the gym, and fresh starchy smells from new blouses and shirts, and pleasant leathery smells from briefcases and brand-new shoes.

"My name is Grace Perkins Jones," said Grace to the girl in the office. "Where should I go?"

The girl looked at her curiously. "Grace Jones? Oh, yes. Your homeroom is Dean Alexander's, number 108 down the hall. She's the dean of girls. Wait a minute! Here's your schedule of classes for the day."

Chapter 2

HERO WORSHIP

All heads turned to look at her. Grace marched up to the teacher's desk and stood at attention, her arms folded on her chest, her feet spread wide apart. "My name is Grace Jones," she said. "I'm supposed to be in this class."

Dean Alexander was an old woman. Her hair was white with blond streaks in it. Her eyes were a faded blue in the middle and yellow where they should have been white, she was so old. The faded eyes looked at Grace. "How do you do, Grace," she said. Then she stood up to survey the room for an empty desk, but before she could choose a desk for Grace she was interrupted by the entrance of another student. All the faces in the classroom stopped staring at Grace and turned to stare at the newcomer. Grace turned to look too, and her jaw dropped in wonder and admiration.

It was a girl. But what a girl! Grace was instantly reminded of Captain Nancy Blackett of *The Flying Cloud*. The girl's hair was cut short like a boy's, like Grace's own hair, and she walked with a hearty athletic step. Captain Nancy would look just like that, and she might even wear clothes like that—what a glorious outfit! The girl was wearing black basketball shoes with rubber cleats, white socks, black stockings, a white blouse, and a pleated tunic of navy-blue serge. It was a uniform of some kind, a splendid uniform.

Her name was Chatty Peak. Dean Alexander introduced her to the class. Everybody seemed to know her already. Chatty had an announcement to make. She stood in the front of the room, her hands resting on her hips with the fingers spraddled forward and the thumbs splayed back. Something glittered on a chain around her neck, flashing sunlight into Grace's eyes, *on*, off, *on*, off, *on*. It was a whistle, a shining silver whistle.

"Hello, everybody," said Chatty Peak. "Welcome to the Winslow S. DeForest School. I guess you all know that I'm the captain of the Girls Leader Corps this year, and on behalf of the Leader Corps and on behalf of Miss Bodecker, the girls' gym teacher, I want to invite all of you girls who are interested in athletics to try out for membership in the Girls

Leader Corps. You're all invited to practice tumbling exercises and basketball shots in the gym every Tuesday and Thursday afternoon after school, beginning next week. The official tryouts will be held on the night of October fifteenth."

A pretty girl in the front row raised her hand. "What does the Girls Leader Corps do anyway, Chatty?" she wanted to know.

Chatty shifted her stance and fingered her whistle, so that it dazzled still more blinding sunshine into Grace's eyes. "Well, Milly Lee, it's kind of a training in leadership and things like that. How to be a good sport. And you help out in the gym and so on and so forth."

"Oh, I see," said Milly Lee.

Chatty nodded briskly at Dean Alexander, bade farewell to the class with a funny little half-military salute, and vanished from the room, her tunic swirling behind her like a Scotsman's kilt.

Grace was stunned. It was hero worship at first sight. Chatty Peak had taken instantaneous possession of the quarterdeck of *The Flying Cloud*. She was Captain Nancy and Captain John rolled into one, and Trueblue Tom was ready to obey her every command. Grace stumbled to the seat pointed out to her by Dean Alexander and sat down with a thump, her head swimming. Then Dean Alexander walked to the door to speak to another teacher, and the classroom immediately squirmed into life.

The boy in front of Grace turned around. He was a tall, broad-shouldered boy with a big nose and a friendly smile. "Hello there, tomboy," he said. "My name's Daniel Margolis. Say, where did you get that stride?"

"Hey, sailor," said the huge fat girl on Grace's right, "are you a boy or a girl?"

"Is it a pirate?" giggled another girl. "Oh, I'm so scared."

Grace was used to this kind of teasing. Ever since she had turned into a tomboy, people had teased her and made jokes about the way she looked. Usually she liked it. She was proud of her short hair and the jaunty nautical cut of her clothes, and it was fun to be looked at and noticed, to make a stir, to have people take it all in. Now she shook her fist amiably, lifted the hinged top of her desk, and put her notebook and pencil case inside.

"Oh, she's a tough one. Did you see that fist?"

"I'll bet she could even beat up Donald Waldorf."

"Look out, Donald. The tomboy's going to get you, Donald."

Everybody was laughing and whispering and looking at Donald Waldorf, a big heavyset boy in the back row. Donald looked surprised.

The whisper went all over the room. "Donald's going to beat up the new girl at lunchtime! Okay, Donald? The girls' hockey field! Is that all right with you, Donald?"

Donald grinned. He didn't say no.

Grace was appalled. She didn't want to fight Donald Waldorf. She hadn't meant to start the school year off like this at all. But Trueblue Tom was consulting his oracles, and of course Captain Nancy and Captain John said fight. "Shiver my timbers!" (That was Captain Nancy.) "If they want a battle, they shall have one! Beasts! Galoots! We'll give it to 'em, broadside to broadside!" Captain John didn't say anything, but his face was grave and he was nodding at his first mate and sticking a pistol into his belt. And, anyway, after hearing what Chatty Peak had said about the Girls Leader Corps, Grace wanted to be a good sport more than anything else in the world. She didn't say no either.

"That will do, class," said Dean Alexander softly, turning away from the door, gathering the reins in her old hands again.

Everyone settled down. Then the bell rang for the beginning of the school day, and Grace consulted her schedule. Her first class was English with Miss Humminger. Then she was to have Math with Mr. Stanley. Then Latin with Dean Alexander. Then lunch in the cafeteria. Lunch, and a battle.

Dutifully Grace went to all her classes and looked at the new books that were handed to her and wrote down her assignments. But she was too nervous to pay much attention. When lunchtime came she hurried to the cafeteria, bought herself a tuna-fish sandwich, sat down at a table by herself, and tried to force the sandwich down. No matter how long she chewed and chewed, each bite was a dry lump that was hard to swallow.

At first she tried to settle her nerves by staring into space and imagining that she was the Lord Admiral of the British fleet and Donald Waldorf was the commander of the Spanish Armada. But this trick didn't work. The commander of the Armada kept turning into a big heavyset boy with arms like iron bands. Donald Waldorf was probably even stronger than Grace's brother Will. Will could always get Grace down on the floor and thwack his bony knees into her shoulders and count to ten before she could even get her breath. Sometimes he even put his hands around her neck and pretended to strangle her for good measure. There were occasions when Will was a noble and dignified older brother, sage and full of wisdom. Other times he was a tyrant.

"Well, how's the pirate?"

It was Daniel Margolis, looming up beside her with a big grin on his face. He had come to fetch her.

Grace swallowed the last lump of her sandwich, pushed back her chair, tugged at her middy, and started for the fray.

Chapter 3

THE
WRESTLING
MATCH

The hockey field was right outside the cafeteria. Girls in green gym suits were rushing up and down the other end of the field brandishing hockey sticks. At the near end of the field stood Donald Waldorf, towering above a milling crowd of onlookers, well-wishers, and curious bystanders.

In spite of Trueblue Tom and Captain Nancy and Captain John, poor Grace was almost overcome with embarrassment. With her heart knocking against her ribs she marched up to Donald Waldorf and came to a solid stop, bracing her sneakers on the parched September grass.

"I don't know how to box," she said. "I just wrestle."

"Well, that's okay, I guess," said Donald Waldorf.

"The first person to get the other person's shoulders down for a count of ten wins," declared Grace.

"Well, okay," said Donald again, agreeably.

The struggle was short and sharp. Donald was taken by surprise. Grace hurled herself at him, knocked him down, fell on top of him, and ground his shoulders into the grass. "One-two-three-four-five-six-seven-eight-nine-TEN," shouted Grace. "I win." Then she stood up with dignity and brushed a few blades of grass from her knees.

The crowd of onlookers was cut off in mid-yell. They all looked at Donald to see if he would contest the decision. But Donald merely got to his feet, rubbed his hair up in the back, grinned, and said "Okay."

Daniel Margolis burst out laughing and clapped Donald on the back. The crowd dispersed. Grace marched back to the cafeteria. She felt terrible, even though she had won. She almost wanted to cry. What did Captain Nancy think? And Captain John? They weren't saying. They didn't even seem to be there. Grace couldn't summon them up from wherever it was they lived, deep down inside. For once she didn't feel like Trueblue Tom at all. She was just a great big dumb stupid girl who had made an awful fool of herself right in front of everybody on her very first day in the Winslow S. DeForest Junior High School.

Well, at least there was one good thing. Chatty Peak hadn't seen her make a fool of herself. Chatty was far away at the other end of the field, showing a bunch of girls how to hold a hockey stick. Grace could tell it was Chatty by her beautiful uniform and by the cut of her short hair.

At the end of the day Daniel Margolis stopped at Grace's locker as she was getting ready to go home. "Guess who likes you?" he said. "Donald Waldorf. He's never liked a girl before. You're the first girl he's ever liked."

Grace laughed and blushed. She was flattered. "Well, shiver my timbers," she said (like Captain Nancy).

Daniel Margolis laughed too, took a pile of books from his locker, and departed.

Grace pulled off her middy, stuffed it into the bottom of her locker, stuck a pencil between her teeth like the cutlass of a pirate, snatched up her books, slammed her locker shut with her knee, and tramped down the hall.

Two teachers were drinking coffee in the teachers' room, and they looked up as Grace went by.

"What a lope that girl has," said Mr. Chester, who taught music and French. "Who's the tomboy?" He got up to watch Grace wham the palm of her hand at a swinging door and charge through it.

"Isn't she a scream?" said Miss Humminger, getting up too, to watch through the window as Grace plummeted down the front steps of the school. "She's in my senior English class. What an *odd* child! Why doesn't she behave like a normal girl? There must be something basically, psychologically wrong with her, deep down inside, don't you think so, Charles? I mean, honestly, *look* at her."

"Well, I don't know," said Mr. Chester. "I rather like her style. Swagger, that's what that girl's got. Real swagger."

"How did you like your first day at school?" said Grace's father, as Grace climbed into the DeSoto.

"It was okay," said Grace. "I'm going to try out for the Girls Leader Corps."

The car was jammed with Grace's father and mother, her big brother Will, her little sister Sophie, and her old bulldog Whitey, who had been part of the family in Ohio and all the way back to the time when the Jones family had lived in Boston, Massachusetts.

"We're on our way to see the new house," said Will. "We've got the key."

"Oh, that's right," said Grace. "I forgot. The new house."

"The new house! The new house!" said Sophie, bouncing up and down on the back seat.

"On to the new house, if you please, Jeeves," said Mrs. Jones, pretending to look through a lorgnette, as if she were none other than Mrs. Winslow S. De-Forest herself.

"Arf-arf!" barked Whitey, excited by the commotion. He climbed up in Grace's lap and licked her face.

Chapter 4

THE
NEW HOUSE

The new house belonged to Mrs. Kane. At first she had not wanted to rent it to Mr. and Mrs. Jones.

"No children," she had said firmly. "Absolutely *no* children."

"But you'll never rent that big house to anybody without children," Mrs. Jones had said.

"One hundred dollars a month," said Mrs. Kane.

"Eighty dollars," said Mrs. Jones.

"Certainly not," said Mrs. Kane.

But in the end Grace's mother had won. Nobody else had wanted to live in a big, rundown, overgrown, lonely place with hardly any neighbors, at the very end of the trolley line. And the house itself looked grim and forbidding. It had been standing empty for two years, ever since Mrs. Kane had been forced to give up the caretaker of her estate, who had been living in it. Now she was in no condition to be choosy. She really needed the money. Her husband had been someone important in the electric power business, but after the big stock market crash in 1929 his business had failed.

"The whole crazy system just caved in of its own weight," explained Grace's father. "And Mr. Kane went with it."

"What happened to him?" Grace wanted to know.

Her mother shook her head. Grace wasn't supposed to hear anything so dark and terrible. Whatever it was, he was dead now. Mrs. Kane was a widow.

But of course the times were still pretty bad for everybody, all over the country. For years, for as long as Grace could remember, people had been saying that the hard times were almost over, that prosperity was just around the corner. Things had been better for awhile, and then everything had collapsed again. Grace's father was one of the lucky ones. His job with the DeForest Company was a good one, even though his pay had been cut three times and he had been transferred twice.

"No pets, of course," Mrs. Kane had said, holding her pen over the lease, frowning at Mrs. Jones.

Grace's mother blinked. "Well, Whitey isn't at all destructive. He's so old he just lies beside the stove and sleeps all the time."

"A dog?" Mrs. Kane looked shocked. "You *do* have a dog?"

"Well, you could hardly call him a dog. He's more like a piece of furniture." Mrs. Jones giggled nervously. "He just lies there and sniffles."

Mrs. Kane had hesitated a moment longer, and then, sighing heavily, she had signed the lease. Mrs. Jones had borne it home in triumph. The house was theirs.

"Not here," said Mrs. Jones, as her husband slowed down and began to turn the car into the driveway between a pair of big stone gateposts. "We're supposed to use the dirt road. Just keep going."

Mr. Jones shifted gears and headed back out onto River Road. "What did you say happened to Mr. Kane?" said Will, turning to look over his shoulder at the long shadowed drive.

"Never you mind," said Mrs. Jones.

The dirt road was less impressive, but it led directly to their new house and to the gardener's cottage. That was rented now too, to a family named Moon.

"Here we are," said Mrs. Jones. "This is the place."

"Say," said her husband, "that's what I call a house."

It was a hodgepodge of brown shingles. With its glowering overhanging roofs it looked like a collection of toadstools springing up in a damp corner, bursting out of the monstrous bushes. A single room exploded out of the top like a taller toadstool or a blunt rocket. The trees around the house had been planted too close, and they shaded the windows heavily. The rusty blue spruces were sixty feet tall. Huge rhododendrons scraped against the black screens shading the porches, and the porches in turn shaded the whole first floor.

The front hall was cast into total darkness. "Isn't that paneling on the walls?" said Grace's father, pleased and proud, as he opened the front door with the key.

They all stretched out their hands and felt the wooden walls, which were coated with sticky varnish, a little damp to the touch.

"Look at that fireplace," said Will. "Look at all those cobblestones."

"I want to see that room in the tower," said Grace. She started running up the stairs.

"Wait for me," shouted Sophie, scrambling after Grace on her short legs.

Will bounded easily past both of his sisters, and managed to be the first to see the funny hexagonal room at the top of the house. "Say," he said, "this is really swell."

There were windows all around, looking out over the treetops to the highway and the Pennsylvania Railroad. And there beyond the tracks lay the Dela-

ware River. Low in the water a big tanker was heading for Philadelphia, and beyond it they could see the dim blue New Jersey shore. The river was dirty and oily close up, they knew that, but from here it looked beautiful and blue.

"Look at all the dead wasps," said Grace, nudging a pile of them with her sneaker.

"Oooooof, it's hot up here," said Sophie.

Then Will found a cool spot. Halfway down the stairs to the second floor there was a low door in the wall. Inside it he discovered the attic storage space. The door and the ceiling were so low they had to crawl in on their hands and knees. It was dank and damp in there, and dark and cool.

"What's that big thing?" said Sophie timidly, pointing at an enormous drum-shaped wooden tub that took up most of the room in the attic.

"I don't know," said Will. He peered over the edge of the tub. "It's full of water. Black, black water. Maybe there's a dead body in there."

"Oh, no," squealed Sophie.

Mrs. Jones was sticking her head in the low door. "He's just joking, Sophie. It's nice clean water. It's where the water is stored to flush the toilets downstairs."

"Oh," said Will. "Well, I still think there could be something dead in there. Like a dead cat."

Sophie scrambled out of the attic in a hurry. "Don't say things like that," said Mrs. Jones. "You know how easy it is to frighten Sophie."

"That's why he does it," said Grace.

They crawled out of the tub-room, clattered down the stairs, looked at the other rooms, and then bolted out the front door to explore the rest of their domain. Eagerly they ran all around the house on the mossy ground under the heavy overhanging trees. Then they followed a path that led past the garage into a hollow filled with towering rhododendrons. The path rose out of the hollow into the sunshine and ran straight along a fence festooned with grapevines. The vines had not been pruned in years, and the long shaggy tendrils trailed right across the path. They were heavy with bunches of blue-black grapes.

What a discovery! Grace and Will and Sophie ate their way along the fence. The grapes were hot from the sun. Will and Sophie spat the sour skins out. Grace let the slippery sweet insides squirt down her throat, and then, wincing, she chewed the skins and swallowed them too.

There was a dirt driveway at the end of the fence. And on the other side of the driveway there was another house. It was a bungalow, a low one-story building made of cobblestones, looking a little like a magic cottage in the middle of the woods. And there on the front porch of the cottage, as if they knew they were part of a fairy story, stood two girls, looking at them, waiting.

"They're new too," whispered Grace.

"I hope there's someone besides girls," grumbled Will.

"Hello there," said the smaller of the two girls.

"Are you the Joneses?" said the bigger one. "Why don't you come on over?"

The Joneses crossed the driveway silently, none of them knowing what to say.

"Cat got your tongues?" said the smaller girl.

Grace shook her head. There was an embarrassed silence.

Then Sophie piped up, and asked a simple, satisfying, stupendous question. "Whatever happened to Mr. Kane?" she said, staring at the smaller girl.

"He shot himself," said the girl cheerfully.

"Oh, is that what he did," said Will.

This horrid news broke the ice, and they all introduced themselves. The two girls were named Moon. Dot was the bigger one. She was Grace's age. Teenie was the smaller one. She was halfway between Grace and Sophie.

"Do you have any brothers?" said Grace, asking the question she knew was uppermost in Will's mind.

"No," said Dot Moon.

"Well, so long," said Will.

"Wait a minute, Will Jones," said Teenie Moon. "Come back here. I want you to meet my teddy bears."

"Your *teddy* bears?" said Will. He snickered, and sauntered off into the grapevine.

"They're not just ordinary bears, Will Jones," shouted Teenie. "They're royal bears. You have to get down on your knees."

"Some other time," yelled Will. He strode off, kicking the grapevines, but his face was red and he was grinning. Grace could tell he thought Teenie Moon was funny.

"Well, hello there, you two," said Mrs. Moon, looking out the screen door. "Girls, why don't you invite your new neighbors inside?"

A long dark hall tunneled through the bungalow. Teenie's room was the first one on the left. She opened the door and pulled Sophie in after her. "Meet my teddy bears, Poncho and Percy," said Teenie. "They expect you to kneel. Here, just get down on your knees on the rug."

Sophie was tickled. She chuckled and got down on her knees. "They're really cute bears," she said.

Grace followed Dot Moon down the long dark hall to the other end. Dot's room was the last one on the left. Grace looked in and stopped cold on the doorsill.

"What's the matter with you?" said Dot. "Come on in."

Hesitantly, timidly, reluctantly, Grace stepped inside. For Trueblue Tom, first mate of *The Flying Cloud*, Dot Moon's room was an alien world.

Chapter 5

THE
PERFUMED
CHAMBER

Grace couldn't believe her eyes. It was everything she hated and despised. It was ruffles and flounces and flowers. There was a dressing table with a ruffled, flounced, flowered chintz skirt. There was a pink, ruffled, flounced, flowered chair with a heart-shaped back. There were bottles and jars and ointments. There were mirrors, and pictures of movie stars.

"What's that thing?" said Grace, pointing at an object on Dot's dressing table.

"It's an eyelash curler," said Dot. "Look, I'll show you how it works." She stuck two fingers into the looped handles of the eyelash curler, leaned over to the three-sided mirror on her dressing table, and squeezed the eyelash curler over her eyelashes. First the right eye, *squeeze*, *squeeze*, and then the left, *squeeze, squeeze.* "There." Dot smiled at Grace and fluttered her eyelids up and down. Her eyelashes stuck straight up. They were bent at the root like the legs of spiders.

"Ugh," said Grace, in horrified fascination.

"Wait a minute. I'm not finished yet," said Dot, giggling, enjoying herself. She squeezed black ooze from a little tube onto a tiny brush, leaned over to the mirror again, and brushed the ooze onto her eyelashes, coating the spider legs with sticky beads of black. The effect was extraordinary. Dot had very beautiful large brown eyes to begin with, and the addition was overwhelming.

"That's horrible," gasped Grace.

"Now for the powder." Dot picked up a pink eiderdown powder puff, dabbed it into a big round box, and then fluffed it over her face. Clouds of powder poufed out of the puff, coating Dot's face with a chalky film of white. Motes of powder floated in the air, falling on the top of the dresser like sweet-smelling dust.

Then Dot picked up an orange lipstick. Pursing her lips carefully she traced a neat outline with the lipstick, then pulled both lips in over her teeth and smacked them together with little popping sounds, to distribute the orange smudge evenly. "Tangee colors your lips the same color they really are," she said.

"Then why use it?" said Grace, almost speechless,

almost overcome by the cheap scent released by the bottles and jars and by the tiny motes of powder that still floated in the air.

The ritual went on. Dot unscrewed a little stopper, and immediately the powerful chemical smell of banana oil billowed out of the bottle. "Nail-polish remover," explained Dot. She sat down lazily on the kidney-shaped stool that belonged to her kidney-shaped dressing table and began brushing the remover over her fingernails with the tiny brush attached to the stopper. Dot's fingernails were bitten down to the quick, and they were blood-red with chipped polish.

Grace sat down on the ruffled, flounced, flowered chair and watched. She didn't know what to say or think. Dot looked so—so—amazing. The flesh-and-blood girl with the pretty face and the candid brown eyes and the pudgy snub nose had become a doll.

"Well, what do you think?" said Dot, fluttering her eyelashes into the mirror at the awed dim face of Grace.

"I think it's disgusting," said Grace. "Absolutely disgusting." Then she said the worst word she could think of. "It's sissy."

"Well, of course it's sissy. Girls are supposed to be sissy. Why do you want to be like a boy?"

Why did she want to be like a boy? There were so many reasons! Grace didn't know where to begin. It was just that girls (ugh!) were so stupid, they were so silly. All they cared about was stupid silly things like clothes and movie stars and chasing boys, or even painting themselves all over with stupid silly powder and lipstick, like Dot. And they never did anything more exciting than maybe take silly stupid piano lessons. Grace herself took piano lessons, but she hated it. Boys were the ones who did all the really interesting things. And they didn't care about silly stupid things like how they looked. They were too busy collecting rocks, like her father, or making radios, like Will, or inventing light bulbs, like Thomas Edison, or flying the Atlantic Ocean, like Charles Lindbergh. And they were faster and stronger than girls. Grace practiced chin-ups every day to develop her biceps, but it was hopeless—she'd never be as strong as Will.

But that was only the half of it. It was books, too. It was Richard Henry Dana's *Two Years Before the Mast,* and Rudyard Kipling's *Captains Courageous,* and above all it was Arthur Ransome's books about the Walker and Blackett children, Captain Nancy Blackett and Captain John Walker and their sisters and brothers, who called themselves the Swallows and Amazons. And it was all the adventures they had, sailing their little boats on a lake in England.

"Have you read Arthur Ransome's *Swallows and Amazons*?" said Grace.

"No," said Dot. "Is that it? Is it because of the

book? Is that why you wear that sailor suit in school? Do you have a boat? Are you really a sailor?"

Grace bit her lip. *Was she really a sailor?* That was an embarrassing question, because in spite of her nautical dreams and visions Grace had never set foot on the deck of a ship. Not even a rowboat. "Well, no," she said. "But my father has promised to take me sailing at Rehoboth Beach. He used to be a sailor. In 1918. In the war."

But Dot was heaving a big book off her dresser, turning the conversation back to literature. "Have you read *Gone with the Wind*?" she said.

"No," said Grace.

"Oh, you should. It's a really well-written book. They've made a movie out of it in Hollywood. Miss Humminger read about it in a movie magazine. It's about this girl in a mansion down south."

"Well, *Swallows and Amazons* is about two families who sail boats on a lake. It's really good too."

Dot looked at Grace critically. She studied Grace's short-clipped hair, and the long straight-cut piece hanging down in Grace's eyes in front. She studied the stiff new dress from Dixie Brothers Dry Goods Store. She examined the too-large sneakers which had once belonged to Grace's brother Will. She looked at the way Grace was sitting on the edge of the chair with her knees far apart and her feet flat on the floor. Then Dot's Tangee-orange lips

widened in a friendly smile.

"That was good," she said, "the way you beat up Donald Waldorf."

The blood rushed to Grace's face. Dot had been there! She had seen it! "Why?" said Grace. "Is he a big bully?"

"Oh, no. He's just a nothing. But it was funny the way you knocked him down. He's supposed to be so strong." Dot stood up and dumped *Gone with the Wind* in Grace's lap. "Here, take it," she said. "It's all yours." And then her generosity went even further. "Want to try my Tangee?" she said.

"What?" said Grace. "Me?"

"Why not? And a little powder? And your hair! Wait! I'll plug in the curling iron!"

"No," cried Grace, springing up from her chair, the big book falling in a heap on the floor. "I have to go back. Good-bye!" She flung herself out the bedroom door, then turned to wave a terrified wild farewell to the flounced and flowered and sweet-scented chamber and to the girl who had become a doll, a pretty doll.

Chapter 6

THE
SEVERAL EYES
OF GOD

"Oh, there you are, Grace." Grace's mother was fumbling in the glove compartment of the DeSoto, looking for something, as Grace came pounding out of the rhododendron bushes beside the garage. "I just want to measure the dining-room windows," said Mrs. Jones. She found her tape measure and hurried back into the house, calling over her shoulder, "We've got to go in a minute."

Beside the kitchen door a clothesline was strung between a pair of iron pipes. The pipes were shaped like the letter U turned upside down. Grace jumped up to one of the pipes, grasped it with both hands and swung for a minute, her toes brushing the ground. The pipe felt just right for chinning. Slowly, with all the strength in her two arms, Grace drew herself up until her chin touched the cold pipe. Then she lowered herself to full stretch. Then she heaved herself up once again.

Captain Nancy was watching Trueblue Tom. "Jib-booms and bobstays, Tom," she said, "you're a man after my own heart."

Captain John was there too, of course, keeping an eye on Trueblue Tom, even though he might look as if he were just tinkering with the donkey engine or weaving two ropes' ends together. "Not half bad," murmured John in his British way, and his praise refreshed Tom's trueblue soul.

She had been right to run from Dot's room, decided Grace. Nancy and John hadn't liked Dot's room either. They had watched her to see whether or not she would do the right thing, and she had. Running away had been the right thing. Grace chinned herself on the iron pipe over and over again, straining and gasping for breath. Once more, now, just once more for Captain Nancy and Captain John.

"Look at her," said Grace's mother. Mrs. Jones was staring at her daughter from the dining-room window. "Just look at that child. She'll get dreadful big muscles, exercising her arms that way. Why does she have to take all this tomboy stuff so *seriously*?"

Mr. Jones looked out the window at Grace too. "Well, that's just the way she is. She always goes overboard. Remember when she thought she was the future queen of England? She gets all worked up. Her imagination runs away with her. Say, will you *look* at that girl. She's getting to be really strong."

"That's what I'm afraid of. Think what they'll look like later on, those big muscles in an evening gown! That child has too much imagination for her own good." Mrs. Jones lifted the window sash. "Grace? Run and get Sophie, will you? There's a good girl."

"Okay," puffed Grace. "Just—one—more—time." Straining mightily, she struggled to bring her chin level with the pipe just once more, failed, hung panting for a moment with her toes touching the grass, then strained upward again, her arms trembling with the effort. This time she managed to graze her chin against the side of the pipe, and she let go at last and dropped triumphantly to the ground. Then she picked herself up and set off for the Moons' house to get Sophie. She could feel her mother's and father's eyes upon her back. They were watching her, she could tell. But it wasn't their eyes that mattered. It was Nancy's and John's. It was their orders she sprang to obey. "Run up aloft, Tom," Captain Nancy was shouting, "to the mains'l yard. Shiver my timbers! Furl the sail before we capsize!"

"Aye, aye, sir," Tom was piping up smartly. And now he was scrambling up the rigging as if it were a flight of steps and running along the yardarm while the ship heeled over in the freshening wind.

"Good lad." That was John, at the wheel, watching Tom haul up the colossal sail and stow it away single-handed. Now the great ship was righting itself and speeding onward, its sleek prow cutting a furrow in the blue waves, the sun casting a bright translucent shadow through the foremast sails on the upturned faces of Captain Nancy and Captain John, who were studying Trueblue Tom, watching every move he made, ready with a quiet word of praise (that was John) or a hearty thump on the back (that was Nancy).

They watched him all the time, Nancy and John, even in the dark, even when Trueblue Tom was asleep in bed. It occurred to Grace as she kicked the long tendrils of the grapevine out of her way along the path to the Moons' bungalow that Nancy and John watched her in exactly the same way that God was supposed to watch people. He was supposed to be able to see everything you did every minute of your life, and judge you for it, and decide whether it was good or bad. John and Nancy were like that. The only difference was that they were real—they were as real to Grace as her mother and father, or Sophie and Will—whereas God—well, Grace wasn't so sure about God. Maybe he was real, and then again maybe he wasn't.

Chapter 7

I
WILL MAKE
MYSELF!

Grace might have had her doubts about Dot Moon, but since they went to the same school they were thrown together whether they liked it or not. On the first school morning after the Joneses had moved into their new house, Dot and Teenie Moon stopped by for Grace, and then the three of them set off for the trolley stop together.

"Where's your brother, Grace Jones?" said Teenie Moon.

"My mother drops off Will and Sophie when she takes my father to work," said Grace. "Their schools are right on the way to the DeForest Building."

"Does your father work for the DeForest Company?" said Dot. "Those DeForests are really rich."

The trolley tracks were at the top of a steep hill. The three girls labored up Bellefonte Street in the raw morning light, struggling past the sad little summer cottages and the miniature abandoned church, stepping over the clumps of grass that grew in the cracks in the pavement. Grace led the way, taking enormous uphill strides to develop her leg muscles for the tryouts for the Girls Leader Corps.

The trolley stop was at the very end of the tracks, at the place where they looped around through a sort of no-man's-land to head back toward town. Grace and Dot and Teenie stood in the tall weeds waiting for the trolley. When it arrived, clanking and rumbling, empty of passengers, it squealed to a stop beside them, and they climbed aboard. They paid the conductor eight cents apiece, and sat down gratefully on the seats of woven straw.

It was a long ride into town, with a squealing, rattling stop every half mile or so to pick up passengers—mostly other students with books in their arms or lady shoppers going into town.

On the trolley Dot told Grace an important thing about the senior class in the Winslow S. DeForest Junior High School. "Do you know about the ring?" she said.

"No," said Grace. "What ring?"

"For Best All-around Girl in the senior class. There's one for the Best All-around Boy too. They give out the rings at the end of the school year. Wouldn't you just love to win the girl's ring?"

"I guess so," said Grace. "Look, what's that long

stone wall with all the broken glass sticking out of the top? We've been going past it for ages."

"Oh, that's where the DeForests live," said Dot. "Mr. and Mrs. Winslow S. DeForest."

"They have some daughters our age," said Teenie.

"Have you ever seen them?" said Grace. "Do they go to our school?"

"Oh, no," said Dot. "They go to private school."

Of course. That was what Grace's mother had said. You couldn't expect rich people to send their children to public school.

The trolley stopped at last at the nearest corner to the Winslow S. DeForest Junior High School, and the three girls jumped down from the shaky metal step, clutching their books to their chests. Then they walked the three blocks to school in the middle of a noisy parade of fellow students. The familiar warm breath of school air enveloped them as Grace dragged on the heavy front door and held it open for Teenie and Dot. Then she said a hurried good-bye to the Moons, ran straight to her locker, jerked it open, yanked out her middy and pulled it down over her dress. There. What a relief! Now she was Trueblue Tom, and she could breathe at last. Poor Tom had been suffocating in the presence of Dot Moon. Somehow Dot's pretty airs and graces flustered him and put him off his stride. But now, with Tom's colors flying at the top of her mainmast and every square inch of her canvas filled with wind,

Grace sailed triumphantly down the corridor. And all the rest of the day she felt like Tom from head to foot, even when she sat next to Dot Moon, even when they walked together from class to class.

They made a funny pair—Grace with her boy's hair flip-flopping over her forehead and her huge baggy navy middy drooping almost to her knees, galumphing along beside pretty Dot, who had a permanent wave and a matching skirt and sweater and a new pair of saddle shoes. Dot wasn't supposed to wear any makeup to school, but Grace could tell by the crook of Dot's eyelashes and the peachy tautness of Dot's cheeks that she had sat in front of her dressing table that morning once again, staring intently into the mirror, powdering and painting herself with the most artistic care.

Grace and Dot had classes together nearly all day long. Even gym. Chatty Peak was in their gym class too, as an assistant to Miss Bodecker. Chatty handed out identical gym suits, like big green rompers, to all the girls in the class, and then Grace and Dot spent the hour rushing all over the hockey field in their new gym suits, their pale thin legs the same shade of bluish white. Neither of them ever got a whack at the ball. They just ran back and forth until they were out of breath, while Chatty Peak whisked the ball up and down the field and whammed it into the net over and over again.

One class Grace didn't share with Dot was Latin,

because Dot was taking French instead of Latin. But Daniel Margolis was in Grace's Latin class. And after class he called her a greasy grind.

"A what?" said Grace. She didn't know whether to be insulted or not.

"You're a greasy grind. You've always got your hand up. Teacher's pet. You're almost as bad as Marjorie Zednick."

"Who's Marjorie Zednick?"

"She's the smartest girl in the school. Always has her hand up. Just like you. Girls make me sick." But Daniel's friendly face was smiling.

"Well, I'm not any good in English," said Grace, trying to sound modest.

It was true. Grace couldn't seem to get the hang of her English teacher, Miss Humminger. Oh, she had done her homework for the day. She had read Wordsworth's poem about daffodils. But in class Miss Humminger had drifted way off the subject. She had sat on the edge of Daniel Margolis's desk and talked about heredity and environment.

"That's what we all are," Miss Humminger had said, shaking her head wisely from side to side. "All of us, ev-er-y sin-gle one of us. We're nothing but a combination of heredity and environment. Heredity is what you inherit from your parents, like a high IQ or athletic ability"—Miss Humminger smiled at Daniel—"and environment is what happens to you afterward, like the training you have as a child, and the schooling you get, and the food you eat, and all that sort of thing. Do you see?"

"But, Miss Humminger," said Grace, raising her hand.

Miss Humminger looked at Grace out of the corner of her eye, wary of the tomboy. "Well, Grace Jones?"

"Isn't there a third thing?" said Grace. "What you do by yourself?"

Miss Humminger smiled indulgently around the class. "No, no, Grace. You may think you are doing something by yourself, but actually it's either because your genes and chromosomes are telling you what to do, or because something in your environment, like something you heard on the radio or saw in the movies, is telling you what to do. Do you see?" Miss Humminger was herself very much influenced by the movies.

Grace couldn't believe it. "No, no, Miss Humminger. I'm sure of it. People can make themselves too." She looked around for agreement. But the others were all shaking their heads.

"I saw a movie last week," said Milly Lee, raising her hand, "and this girl, it was Deanna Durbin, she had her hair parted in the middle, and I went home and parted my hair in the middle too, and that's why I always part it in the middle now." Milly turned this way and that to display her environmental characteristic.

"Daniel Margolis has ears that stick out like Clark Gable's," said Ruth Marshall. Ruth was an overweight girl who secretly admired Daniel. Everyone laughed, including Daniel, who put his hands over his ears and pretended to be squashing them back.

"No, no," laughed Miss Humminger. "Daniel inherited his ears from his parents. That's heredity, not environment."

"But, don't you see," cried Grace, half standing up, she was so excited, "don't you *see*? It doesn't matter what your parents were, or what they or anybody else try to turn you into, you can be somebody by yourself, you can be anybody you want to, you can make yourself."

"Perhaps *you* can, Grace Jones," said Miss Humminger sarcastically. "But as for the rest of us, it's just a wee bit difficult."

Everybody laughed at Grace, and she turned red and stopped talking. But in her mind she didn't give up. I don't care, she said to herself stubbornly. I can make myself. I will, I will. And they can't stop me.

She argued it out with Dot in the cafeteria. Dot had fallen hook, line, and sinker for Miss Humminger's theory.

"But I'm making myself, I know I am," said Grace, feeling Trueblue Tom inside her hoisting sail, hauling on the rope with all his might.

"You just think you are," said Dot comfortably. "What makes you a tomboy? Those books you read, that's all."

"No, no, it's more than that. I know it is."

"Well, what is it then?"

But Grace couldn't say what it was that made it more. And she was still struggling with the problem when she got up from the table to go to orchestra practice. (Orchestra practice! She had to admit to herself that she certainly wasn't making herself right now. Her environment, in the shape of her mother, was pushing her around. Grace was only joining the orchestra because her mother wanted her to.)

The orchestra conductor was Mr. Chester. He looked up as Grace stalked down the sloping aisle of the auditorium, and then he stood with his mouth open, watching her come into port, taking long strides with the downward flow of gravity. Awe-inspired, he studied Grace hopefully. If ever a young female looked as if she could play the tuba, it was this one. The orchestra needed a tuba player.

Mr. Chester pointed at Grace with a lordly sweep of his baton. "And what instrument do you play, Captain Bligh?" he said.

Mr. Chester was terribly good-looking. Grace looked up at him shyly, feeling a certain inward spark in response to Mr. Chester's steely blue eyes and wavy brown hair, but Trueblue Tom instantly stamped out the spark with his big sneaker. "I play the piano," she said.

"Oh, no," groaned Mr. Chester, "not another

piano player. I don't suppose you're any good at it, by any chance?"

"No, I'm not," said Grace honestly.

"Well, all right. Sit down at the piano and let's all take a whack at *Liebestraum*. The piano part is just a lot of C-major chords."

Finding her way to the piano, Grace had to squeeze past Donald Waldorf's big bass viol. Donald's face turned red. He didn't say a word, he just smiled. Grace decided Donald Waldorf was just shy. She sat down at the piano and took a look at her music. The first page was all C-E-G-C. It didn't look too bad.

Mr. Chester raised his baton and explained the music. "This is supposed to be a dream of love," he said. "Ready? Now then! *ONE*-two-three! *ONE*-two—"

Ka-*BANG*! thundered Grace at the piano.

Mr. Chester lowered his arms and looked at his piano player. "Listen, Captain Bligh," he said. "You're not firing the ship's cannon, you're dreaming of love."

"Sorry," said Grace.

All the other girls in the orchestra tittered and blushed. *They* knew what a dream of love meant. They were all in love with Mr. Chester.

After school Mr. Chester met Miss Humminger in the teachers' room again, and again they discussed the new tomboy.

"The child's so strange," said Miss Humminger.

"Oh, do you think so?" said Mr. Chester. "Actually, I find her rather amusing." Part of Mr. Chester's power over women came from his imperious habit of disagreeing with everything they said.

"But she's abnormal," insisted Miss Humminger.

"I wonder if she has a tree?" mused Mr. Chester. "Every tomboy should have a favorite tree."

"Well, I'd just like to get my hands on her and fix her up," said Miss Humminger.

"Oh, dear no, Adelaide. Just let her alone. I rather like her the way she is."

Mr. Chester strolled away down the hall, and Miss Humminger, after admiring his retreating back until it disappeared around the corner, sighed heavily, and walked across the corridor to her own classroom to grind out the next day's homework assignment for her senior English class.

Miss Humminger didn't know it, but this homework assignment was a bombshell. Tomorrow it would become a part of the environment of every member of her senior English class, and of course this was true of all of Miss Humminger's assignments. But in the case of one of her students, the tomboy, Grace Jones, this new piece of environment was destined to combine or intertwine or collide with a lot of Grace's inherited characteristics, and go off with a tremendous wallop.

Chapter 8

AN
INCENSE-BEARING
TREE

Miss Humminger's English assignment was folded in Grace's notebook when she discovered her tree. Dot and Teenie Moon had decided to go shopping after school, so Grace had taken the trolley home alone. After galloping down the hill to River Road she had turned to the left on a sudden impulse, and headed for the grand stone gateposts that led to Mrs. Kane's big house. She had never been back there, and she wanted to see what it was like.

The afternoon was cloudy and moist, threatening rain. The long paved drive, pitted with potholes, crumbling into weeds at the edges, led directly to Mrs. Kane's great stone house, but Grace soon ducked behind the box hedge and found a secluded path made of stepping stones. To her delight the path brought her to a series of small gardens dropping down the hillside in the direction of the river. If the old gardener could have seen them he would have been heartbroken, but Grace was entranced by the sprawling chrysanthemums and the jungle of rose briers reaching out to claw at her as she picked her way along the path. Glittering golden-green Japanese beetles crawled on the orange and yellow and blood-red roses, and huge ragged blossoms burst at her touch and showered their petals on the ground.

Beyond the rose garden lay a lily pond, half choked with weeds. A multitude of coarse green lily pads on strong rubbery stems lifted their cups above the dank water. As Grace came near there was a sudden splashing noise, *kerplunk*. A frog! Oh, where was he? Grace ran across the little stone bridge and crouched down on the shore to look for him, but he was gone. *Kerplunk, kerplunk*. More frogs! Oh, why couldn't she see them? They flopped into the water before she could get anywhere near.

The lily pond was the end of the formal part of the garden. Beyond it a grassy lane curved around and led back up the hill, ending in a field of tall grass and weeds and Queen Anne's lace. And in the middle of the field there was a white pine tree.

It looked enormous in the mist. The great trunk rose endlessly, lifting and spreading its irregular branches very wide and very high, bristling with broken snags. Impulsively, Grace stuffed her notebook into the bottom of her sailor middy and pulled the drawstring tight. The top of the tree looked like a great place to do her homework.

She began to climb. It was easy. Branches and snags presented themselves readily to her groping hands and feet, and she was soon high in the tree, leaning comfortably and securely against the black column of the trunk, one arm wrapped around the main stem, one foot safely wedged into a crotch, the other dangling.

From there she could see the rooftops of Mrs. Kane's house. She could see the pink asbestos roof of the Moons' bungalow. She could see the squat skyrocket on the top of her own house. She could even, she was sure of it, smell the delicate light fragrance of the roses in the rose garden, mingling with the strong dark scent of the pitch that blackened her fingers. The fog lay cushioned on the dead flower heads of the Queen Anne's lace, on the heavy bending blades of grass, on the bushy foliage of the shaggy trees. It lay beading on the oily surface of River Road, darkening the clammy stones of the ragged wall, touching, misting, touching the silver surface of the pond. A scattering of gray birds flew silently through the gray air and came to rest in a shadowy gray tree far away. Grace saw everything. She noticed everything. She stood transfixed, aware of a spell she could not name.

The tree moved slightly at her back like the mast of a ship gently swaying as the prow dipped into the

hollows of the waves. She was high above the deck in the crow's nest, far out to sea. And Trueblue Tom was standing his watch, scanning the horizon for a coral reef, or a sight of land, or a glimpse of a threatening black sail along the Coast of Barbary. Dreamily, Grace reached into the front of her middy and pulled out Miss Humminger's mimeographed sheets. Then, idly, carelessly, she began to read the poem printed in blurry purple ink on the first page.

> *In Xanadu did Kubla Khan*
> *A stately pleasure-dome decree:*
> *Where Alph, the sacred river, ran*
> *Through caverns measureless to man*
> *Down to a sunless sea.*

Grace drank it in. The poem was one with the tree and the mist, one with the frogs and the lily pads in the pond.

> *So twice five miles of fertile ground*
> *With walls and towers were girdled round:*
> *And there were gardens bright with sinuous rills,*
> *Where blossomed many an incense-bearing tree;*
> *And here were forests ancient as the hills,*
> *Enfolding sunny spots of greenery.*

Halfway through she began murmuring the words to herself aloud.

The shadow of the dome of pleasure
Floated midway on the waves;
Where was heard the mingled measure
From the fountain and the caves.
It was a miracle of rare device,
A sunny pleasure-dome with caves of ice!

A damsel with a dulcimer
In a vision once I saw:
It was an Abyssinian maid,
And on her dulcimer she played,
Singing of Mount Abora.

. . . .

I would build that dome in air,
That sunny dome! those caves of ice!
And all who heard should see them there,
And all should cry, Beware! Beware!
His flashing eyes, his floating hair!
Weave a circle round him thrice,
And close your eyes with holy dread,
For he on honey-dew hath fed,
And drunk the milk of Paradise.

Dizzy with incantation, intoxicated with rhythm, Grace almost fell out of the tree. She had discovered poetry and nature in one fell swoop. "Beware," she whispered to herself, "Beware! Beware! Weave a circle round him thrice. . . ." Then her eyes raced back to the beginning of the poem, and she started to read the whole thing aloud once more, mumbling and whispering at first, then ranting and shouting—

> *In Xanadu did Kubla Khan*
> *A stately pleasure-dome decree . . .*

By the time Grace noticed her dog Whitey at the bottom of the tree, sniffling and whining a doggy greeting, the two mimeographed pages in her hand were a damp smudge of purple ink. She never discovered the questions Miss Humminger had typed up on the second page, but she wouldn't have been able to read them anyway, they were so blurred by now. But she knew the whole poem by heart. She slipped and fumbled down the tree, fondled Whitey, staggered home, burst into the kitchen door, struck a pose, and cried, "Beware! Beware! My flashing eyes! My floating hair!"

Grace's mother looked up from her ironing in surprise. "Why, Grace," she said, "I hope you haven't been wearing that sloppy thing in school. Where have you been? You're soaking wet."

"Exploring," said Grace, waving one arm in the direction of the garden and the white pine tree. "It's really pretty over there."

Chapter 9

MISS HUMMINGER
DRINKS
THE MILK OF PARADISE

"Grace Jones," said Miss Humminger, "do you have the answer to the first question in the Samuel Taylor Coleridge assignment for today? Who was Kubla Khan? What was his historical significance?"

Grace was taken aback. She groped for an answer. "Well, I guess he was the one who built a pleasure-dome where Alph the sacred river ran through caverns measureless to man down to a sunless sea?"

"Didn't you look up Kubla Khan in the encyclopedia? Well, perhaps you are better prepared for the second question. Do you happen to know the circumference of Kubla Khan's real-estate development?"

After a moment's thought Grace recited brightly, "So twice five miles of fertile ground with walls and towers were girdled round!"

"And what, pray tell, is *twice* five miles?"

Grace gaped at Miss Humminger, her mind awash with the rhythms of Coleridge's magic verse, her face empty and blank.

"How many miles, class, is twice five miles?"

"Ten miles," giggled the class.

"Of what vegetable species, Dorothy Moon, is honeydew a member? Does it contain seeds or pits? Where is it grown? Of what country is it the principal commercial product?"

"The melon family," said Dot promptly, giving Grace an apologetic look. "It contains seeds. It is grown in California and Georgia. It is a principal product of Italy."

"Very good, Dorothy. Tomorrow, class, we will discuss another poem by Samuel Taylor Coleridge, *The Ancient Mariner*. You will find it in your textbook, beginning on page thirty-two."

The ice cream in the cafeteria came in paper Dixie cups. Teenie Moon carried her Dixie cup to the table where her sister Dot was sitting with Grace Jones, and plunked it down. "Who have you got today, sister dear?" she said.

"I'll see," said Dot. She took hold of the tab on the lid of her Dixie cup and pulled the lid off. Then she licked the ice cream from the underside and peeled off the thin paper that protected the picture of the movie star. "Clark Gable," said Dot. "Oh, good. He's the kind I go for. He's the kind that sweeps you off your feet. Who have you got?"

Teenie and Grace licked their Dixie cup lids and peeled off the paper. "Gary Cooper," said Teenie. "He's the strong silent type. He just says yup and nope." Teenie grinned at Grace. "That's the kind Grace likes. Donald Waldorf! He's the strong silent type!"

"Oh, I do not," protested Grace hotly.

"Oh, everybody knows about you and Donald," laughed Dot. She was making the whole thing up. Donald had never spoken a word to Grace, nor she to him, since the day Grace had beaten him up. He was strong, all right, and silent, all right. He just sat in the back row and never opened his mouth.

Grace was furious with Dot. "You make me so mad," she said.

"Oh, look, Grace," said Dot. "Yours is Olivia de Haviland. She's the beautiful noble type. She should be in a movie with Gary Cooper. The strong silent type always goes for the beautiful noble type." Dot put the two Dixie cup lids side by side. "Gary Cooper is the type that would never propose to you. He's too shy. You'd have to propose to him."

Teenie snatched at the chance to pick on her sister. "If *you* proposed to Gary Cooper," she said, "you know what he'd say? 'Nope,' that's what he'd say. You want to know why? Because you've got a big nose, that's why."

"Oh, you shut up," said Dot angrily.

Grace pushed her chair back and stood up. She was feeling gloomy after her failure in English class, and the conversation at the table was hateful to Trueblue Tom. Oh, Tom liked going to the movies all right, but it was beneath his dignity to talk about movie stars. Grace walked over to the wall to read once again a notice pinned to the bulletin board. It was signed by Chatty Peak, and it was just like the speech Chatty had given in Grace's class on the first day of school. Grace had read the notice every day since then.

GIRLS WHO WANT TO TRY OUT FOR MEMBERSHIP IN THE GIRLS LEADER CORPS SHOULD SIGN UP BELOW AND REPORT FOR PRACTICE IN THE GYM ON TUESDAY, SEPTEMBER 25, AFTER SCHOOL.
(signed) Chatty Peak, Captain, Girls Leader Corps

"Barbecued billy goats!" Captain Nancy had said when Grace had read the notice for the first time. "Sign, Tom, my lad, sign!"

So Grace had signed up at once, and by now she knew the text of the notice by heart. But it still made her heart beat with anxiety and anticipation. Would she pass the trials or wouldn't she? Grace yearned to be a member of the Girls Leader Corps. Maybe if she were really a member she would get to know Chatty Peak. So far Grace had not even had a chance to say hello, because the fabulous Chatty

58

was always moving too fast—running around the school in her uniform, doing errands for Miss Bodecker, refereeing hockey games, blowing her silver whistle with piercing shrieks in gym class or out on the field. She never seemed to stay in one place long enough to be talked to.

Grace stared at Chatty's signature on the notice until the image of Chatty and her silver whistle melted and blurred and blended into the poem Grace had learned the day before—

> *A damsel with a dulcimer*
> *In a vision once I saw:*
> *It was an Abyssinian maid,*
> *And on her dulcimer she played,*
> *Singing of Mount Abora.*

Chapter 10

A VISIT
WITH
THE MOONS

The next Coleridge bombshell lay in Grace's lap, hidden away between pages thirty-two and forty-eight of her English book, as she sat on the straw seat of the trolley car on the way home. But Grace hadn't discovered it yet. She was still lost in dreams of the Girls Leader Corps. Jiggling and jerking with the motion of the trolley, staring vaguely out the window at the DeForests' mile-long stone wall, she was really seeing something else—a vision of True-blue Tom on the night of the official tryouts. He was executing amazing feats of gymnastic skills before the wondering eyes of Chatty Peak—tricks he had practiced while hanging by his knees from the yard-arm, or shinnying up the mizzenmast of *The Flying Cloud*.

Dot was silent too. Usually she chattered all the

way home about Milly Lee's latest angora sweater or which boys she thought were cute or who was going to get the ring for being the best all-around girl or boy or the mean things Scarlett O'Hara did to Rhett Butler in *Gone with the Wind*. But today Dot seemed downcast and withdrawn.

But Dot's sister Teenie was in high spirits. She was a mine of funny stories about the teachers.

"We had Mr. Chester in study hall today," said Teenie, "and he told us he has less than an eighth of an inch of fat over the entire surface of his body."

"You made that up," snapped Dot.

"No, no, it's really true. He was as red as a lobster and he said he had a massage under the sunlamp at the Y, and the coach at the Y told him he had less than an eighth of an inch of fat over the entire surface of his—"

"Oh, stop," said Dot.

"He's cute, though, you have to admit that," said Teenie. "Oh, Grace Jones, how's your brother? Tell him I think he's just awful."

Teenie was always asking Grace about Will. She pretended she thought he was awful, and Will pretended he thought Teenie was a stupid little kid, but he never seemed to mind when she came over and hung around. Grace just couldn't understand it.

"Okay," said Grace, "I'll tell him."

"And tell him I'm coming over with my teddy bears and make him kneel down."

Grace laughed in spite of herself. Teenie and her teddy bears! Teenie was much too old for stuffed animals, but she didn't play with them like toys— she used them as a form of power. And today, when the three girls had jumped off the trolley at the end of the line and trudged down the hill to the dirt road and the driveway in front of the Moons' house, Teenie turned on her bear-power once again.

"Grace Jones," she commanded, "you come right in this house with me. Poncho and Percy demand your humble presence. They will not be disobeyed."

"Oh, all right," said Grace good-naturedly, "just this once." Teenie was a pest, it was true, but there was something comical about her all the same. Everything she did was funny somehow, even the way she talked, even her voice, which had a cheerful grown-up note of drollery in it that sounded strange coming from a skinny little girl with a budlike face and a Buster Brown haircut. Grace tumbled her books on the porch steps and followed the two Moons into the house. Dot drifted away down the long dark hall, and Grace marched into Teenie's room. Teenie slammed the door behind her and pulled the chain across with a *rattle-bang*. Then she walked across the braided rug and stood at attention beside her teddy bears.

"Pay homage, miserable peasant, to their illustrious majesties, Poncho and Percy," she said.

The big white bear, Poncho, had lost some of his

stuffing, and he leaned limply against Percy on the windowsill. A good deal of Percy's brown fur had been rubbed off.

"Greetings and salutations, Poncho and Percy," said Grace.

"Kiss them on the nose."

"No, I won't."

"Grace Jones, you get down on your knees and beg their forgiveness. Say you're sorry. You have hurt their royal feelings."

"Oh, I'm terribly sorry, Poncho. I'm terribly sorry, Percy," said Grace, thumping herself down on the rug on her knees.

"That's better."

"Well, I have to go now. So long, Teenie."

"You can't go until Poncho and Percy declare this royal audience at an end. Your majesties, may the lowly peasant depart? Okay, they say it's okay."

Grace started for the door.

"STOP! You've got to bow! You've got to bow first! Walk backward! You must never turn your back on royal bears! Good-bye, Grace Jones!"

BANG! The door slammed behind Grace, and the bolt clattered across with a crash.

Grace started for the front door. But then she was waylaid once again. There beside her was Dot, looming up palely in the dark hallway, crooking her finger urgently at Grace. "Grace? Could you come in my room for a minute? Just one little minute?"

"Well, all right, but I've got to get going pretty soon."

Grace followed Dot down the dark tunnel to the other end of the hall. BANG! The door of Dot's room slammed behind them. Dot shot the bolt to. *Rattle-bang.*

Once again Grace was trapped. Dot gestured at the ruffled chair and made her sit down. Then she stood in front of Grace and leaned forward, her beautiful brown eyes staring anxiously into Grace's face. "Now, Grace," she said, "I want you to be honest. Ab-so-lute-ly honest. I want you to swear you will tell me the honest truth. Do you swear?"

"Well, sure, okay."

"Tell me, Grace, honestly, I mean, really. Tell me the truth. Do I have a big nose?"

Grace opened her mouth in surprise.

"No, no, wait!" cried Dot. "Just a minute. I mean it, I really mean it. The truth. Don't lie to me, Grace. I can take it. I do, don't I? I really do have a big nose!"

"No, you don't have a big nose," said Grace, wondering if she were lying or not. "You have a nice middle-sized nose. It isn't big, really it isn't."

"Oh, come on, Grace," said Dot, her face white. "I don't want you to be nice. I want you to be honest. I want you to tell me the *truth*." Dot took hold of Grace and shook her. "The TRUTH! I have a big nose! I do! I know I do!"

"No, no," cried Grace, "you don't either. REALLY. I mean, I'm *really* telling the truth. You don't have a big nose!"

"The TRUTH," shouted Dot. She snatched up the hand-mirror from her dressing table and stared at herself in it. "LOOK at that nose. It's BIG! Anybody can see that my nose is big. You couldn't POSSIBLY call that nose a middle-sized nose. I have a great—big—nose." Dot's eyes began to fill with tears.

Grace wanted to get away. "Of course it's not small and *sharp* like some," she said cleverly. "It's *soft*. It's a nice *soft* nose."

"Soft?" repeated Dot, staring at her nose in the mirror.

"It's a nice soft middle-sized nose."

"It's true, it's not pointed or sharp or hooked, or anything," said Dot, smiling gently, staring back at her beautiful eyes in the mirror.

"It's not big at all," said Grace, getting up carefully.

"No, it's more soft," agreed Dot. She picked up the curling iron that was plugged into the lamp socket and began frizzing her hair.

"Well, so long," said Grace, unlatching the door quietly and easing herself out.

"So long," murmured Dot, staring at herself with a dreamy smile. A thin thread of smoke rose from the curling iron and a faint burning smell mingled with the perfume of face powder and nail polish.

Grace shook her head and hurried down the tunnel toward the light of day, thanking her stars that she was Trueblue Tom. *Tom* didn't care if his nose was as big as a light bulb and all covered with warts. Not Tom. What silly stupid *dopes* girls were!

Chapter 11

THE CURSE
IN A
DEAD MAN'S EYE

The Ancient Mariner was even more staggering than *Kubla Khan*. There wasn't the slightest breeze moving in the top of the white pine tree, but Grace had to hang on with both arms to the branches on either side of her to keep from losing her balance, as Coleridge's verses reeled and throbbed, ebbed and flowed across the pages of the book wedged open in her lap. The ancient mariner had shot a lucky bird, an albatross, with his crossbow, and ever since then his ship had been doomed with a curse. And what a curse! All the other sailors died, one by one, and after that he was alone.

> *Alone, alone, all, all alone,*
> *Alone on a wide, wide sea!*
> *And never a saint took pity on*
> *My soul in agony.*

The many men, so beautiful!
And they all dead did lie:
And a thousand thousand slimy things
Lived on; and so did I.

. . . .

An orphan's curse would drag to hell
A spirit from on high;
But oh! more horrible than that
Is the curse in a dead man's eye!

There was something about the rhythm. It burned
and froze. It beat and pulsed. It surged and dragged.
It made Grace want to laugh and cry.

All in a hot and copper sky,
The bloody Sun, at noon,
Right up above the mast did stand,
No bigger than the Moon.

Day after day, day after day,
We stuck, nor breath nor motion;
As idle as a painted ship
Upon a painted ocean.

Water, water, everywhere,
And all the boards did shrink;
Water, water, everywhere,
Nor any drop to drink.

> *The very deep did rot: O Christ!*
> *That ever this should be!*
> *Yea, slimy things did crawl with legs*
> *Upon the slimy sea.*

The tree behind Grace's back was still the crow's nest of *The Flying Cloud*, but that tidy ship was no longer tacking sensibly south southwest in the general direction of Cape Horn. Trueblue Tom and his captains stood awestruck and silent upon a deck that was heaving and swelling upon a far, far different sea. And from now on it was the wild landscape of *The Ancient Mariner* that was to be the natural horizon of *The Flying Cloud*—

> *The Sun's rim dips; the stars rush out:*
> *At one stride comes the dark;*
> *With far-heard whisper, o'er the sea,*
> *Off shot the spectre-bark.*

Grace began to learn this poem by heart too. It was easy. The verses beat themselves into her brain like hammerblows, leaving deep dents in her memory. By the time she was ready to climb down from the top of the tree and stumble home, stiff with cold, the dry grass of the field, like a dull mirror, was giving back the tawny color of the sunset sky. She had memorized forty-two stanzas. And that night at home she learned forty more while she was eating her supper and washing the dishes.

"*I took the oars*," cried Grace, sloshing a plate up and down in the dishpan, "*I took the oars, I took the oars*—wait a minute, wait a minute, how does the next line go?" She held the wet plate dripping over the floor and ran a wet finger over the page of her book. "*The Pilot's boy*, why can't I remember that?

> *I took the oars: the Pilot's boy,*
> *Who now doth crazy go,*
> *Laughed loud and long, and all the while*
> *His eyes went to and fro.*
> *'Ha! ha!' quoth he, 'full plain I see*
> *The Devil knows how to row."*

Grace laughed insanely for the Pilot's boy, and then tossed the plate to Will with a wild sweep of her arm.

Will wasn't ready. "Hey, hey," he said, as the dish fell with a smash on the floor.

"Oh, really, Grace," said her mother crossly. "Now, you clean that up. And please be more careful."

"Di-da-da-dit," mumbled Will. He was learning the Morse code. He had his own book leaning up against the dish-drainer. "Di-da-da-dit is P. Di-da-da-dit is P."

Sweeping the broken pieces of the plate into the dustpan, Grace ranted on—

'O shrive me, shrive me, holy man!'
The hermit crossed his brow.
'Say quick,' quoth he, 'I bid thee say—
What manner of man art thou?'

Grace's father was leaning back in his chair at the kitchen table, sipping his coffee, puffing his after-dinner cigar. "It just so happens that I know a few fragments of the world's great verse myself," he said. And he began to recite *Abou Ben Adhem.* Grace had heard it before.

Abou Ben Adhem—may his tribe increase!—
Awoke one night from a deep dream of peace,
And saw, within the moonlight in his room,
Making it rich and like a lily in bloom,
An angel writing in a book of gold.
Exceeding peace had made Ben Adhem bold,
And to the presence in the room he said:
"What writest thou?" The vision raised its head,
And with a look made of all sweet accord,
Answered, "The names of those who love the Lord."
"And is mine one?" said Abou. "Nay, not so,"
Replied the angel. Abou spoke more low,
But cheerily still; and said: "I pray thee, then,
Write me as one that loves his fellow-men."
The angel wrote, and vanished. The next night
It came again with a great wakening light,
And showed the names whom love of God had blessed,
And lo! Ben Adhem's name led all the rest.

72

He stood up and bowed, but no one had been listening. Grace's mother was on the telephone, Sophie was reading a Mickey Mouse funny-book, Will was mumbling di-di-da's, and Grace had her nose back in *The Ancient Mariner*. "I pass, like night!" she shouted, throwing back her head and closing her eyes to avoid the temptation of looking at the book again—

> *I pass, like night, from land to land;*
> *I have strange power of speech;*
> *That moment that his face I see,*
> *I know the man that must hear me:*
> *To him my tale I teach!*

"Well, Whitey," said Grace's father good-humoredly, addressing the dog, "since nobody appreciates a man of culture and refinement, I guess I'll go down to the cellar and see how the furnace is doing on its first day on the job. It looks like a cold night." He thumped down the cellar stairs and began shoveling more coal into the maw of the giant furnace. Rattling noises came up through the floor. The kitchen radiator hissed and banged. Steam was building up pressure in it for the first time. Grace's mother came into the kitchen with a giant roll of cellophane.

"What's that for?" said Will.

"I'm going to tape it over the inside of the windows, to keep the cold out."

"You mean," said Will cleverly, "to keep the heat *in*."

"Well, whichever it is." Mrs. Jones stood on a chair, held the roll of cellophane up against the window and cut off a piece that was just the right length. Then she began attaching it to the window frame all the way around with sticky tape. Tiny breezes trapped behind it billowed and whispered, and the window glittered strangely.

"Say, that really works," said Will, holding his hand up to a place where the tape wasn't quite stuck down. "Feel that cold air."

"Bedtime, Sophie," said Grace's mother, getting down off the chair.

"Oh, no," said Sophie, looking up from her funny-book. "I don't want to go to bed." She opened her mouth wide and began to howl.

"Why, Sophie," said her mother, "whatever is the matter?"

"The slimy things," wept Sophie. "The slimy things with legs."

"But, Sophie," said Grace, "it's just a poem. You know it's just a poem."

Just a poem or not, it had been too much for Sophie. She was afraid of the slimy things that crawled with legs upon the slimy sea, and the curse in a dead man's eye and the Nightmare Life-in-Death who thicks man's blood with cold. "I'm scared," sobbed Sophie. "I don't want to go to bed."

"Now, Grace," said her mother, "just see what you've done. Just keep your scary poems to yourself hereafter, do you hear?"

"Well, all right," said Grace, crestfallen.

Grace had a little trouble getting to sleep herself that night. She lay looking up at the cold moon, which was sailing high in the night sky, sucking the summer warmth from the ground, casting a cold, bald light on the floor beside the bed. The radiator hissed and knocked. The powerful rhythms of *The Ancient Mariner* were still tumbling and racing through her head. She couldn't stop them. After the third time through all of the eighty-four stanzas she had learned that day she sat up wearily, turned away from the window, and stared wide-eyed at the darkest corner of her room, where the open door into the hall cast a dense shadow. What if an angel should appear there, writing in a book of gold? Was it true that someone was keeping track? Watching her? Writing it all down on the good or bad side of the page? That would be terrible. It would be much worse to have an angel watching her than Captain Nancy and Captain John, because Nancy and John were her friends, after all, and they weren't writing it all down like that and holding a lot of things against her forever after.

Grace kept her eyes pricked open, staring as hard as she could at the dark corner, trying by sheer force of will to materialize an angel writing in a book of gold. But she couldn't do it, and she slumped back under the covers.

Was it true? Were angels true? Was God true? Grace wondered about God for the thousandth time. Her father didn't believe in religion. He scoffed at the Sunday morning preachers on the radio. He always said the word "God" sarcastically, so that it came out "*Gawd*." But Grace didn't know whether he was right or not. What if he were wrong? Somebody in the family should take some responsibility about religion. Just in case it *was* true. Somebody, *somebody*, should pray for everybody. Grace shut her eyes and put her folded hands under her chin, and prayed for them all (just in case), ending up with a line from *The Ancient Mariner*, " 'O, shrive me, shrive me, holy man!' Amen."

BANG! exploded the radiator. *Bubblety-gurglety-poppety-BANG!*

How could a person *ever* get to sleep? Grace opened her eyes wearily, and stared into the dark corner. Then she choked in startled horror. The angel! There was a white shape like an angel in the corner! But instead of writing in a book of gold, the angel made a whimpering noise and landed in Grace's bed with one giant leap. It was Sophie, throwing her arms around Grace's neck in a strangling grip. "The radiator!" gasped Sophie. "The slimy things! The slimy things with legs! They're in the radiator!"

"There, there, Sophie. It's just the hot steam in the pipes. You know it's just the steam." Grace hugged Sophie until she stopped whimpering and shivering. Then Grace, exhausted, settled down too, and closed her eyes, glad to snuggle against a warm sister. Now the two of them were safe against the Nightmare Life-in-Death and the curse in a dead man's eye, and even against the angel writing in the book of gold.

Chapter 12

THE
TRYOUTS

The practice sessions before the tryouts for the Girls Leader Corps began the next day, and continued every Tuesday and Thursday for six weeks. All the girls who had signed up for the tryouts came faithfully to the gym after school to work on their tumbling exercises and their basketball shots under the guidance of Chatty Peak and Miss Bodecker, the gym teacher. The other members of the Girls Leader Corps were there too, every time, to help the earnest candidates for membership—holding their legs up in the air while they stood on their heads, catching them at the end of the double-roll, giving them helpful hints on shooting baskets. The uniforms of the Leader Corps were very much in evidence, because all the girls who were lucky enough to be members wore them every chance they got.

78

But only Chatty Peak had a whistle. All the long hours Grace spent in the gym that fall were punctuated by the shrill blasts of Chatty's shining whistle. Chatty would stand on the sidelines during a game of basketball, acting as the referee with her feet spread apart, her elbows akimbo, her thumbs splayed back and her fingers spread forward on her hipbones like a boy, her shoulders drooping with an athletic sort of slouch. Grace was sure the two of them would have a lot of things in common if they could ever get to be friends. But she couldn't imagine ever getting up the courage to speak to the famous important celebrated Chatty Peak. Once she had found herself standing beside Chatty at a basketball practice just before the Leader Corps tumbling exercises were to begin in the gym. Grace had felt her face grow hot as she struggled to think of something to say. Then she knew. Chatty Peak was a kind of living, breathing Captain Nancy Blackett, and Grace had often wondered whether Chatty knew about her literary counterpart. She came out at last with a timid question, after rehearsing it under her breath.

"Did you ever read *Swallows and Amazons*?" she said, in a voice that was fainter and timider than she had intended.

"What?" said Chatty absently, her eyes fastened on the basketball players.

Grace cleared her throat and tried to speak louder. "I said, did you ever read—"

Breeeeeeeeeeeeeeeeeeeeeeep! Breeeeep! Breeeeeep! Breeeeeeep! Chatty was blowing her whistle imperiously. She was out in the middle of the floor, jerking the basketball from one of the girls, holding it over her head. "Foul, Miss Bodecker," she said briskly. "Martha Manning was offside."

Martha Manning blushed. "I'm sorry, Chatty. I— I didn't know I was so close."

Chatty blew her whistle again, *breeeeeeep!* to start the action, tossed the ball up between the two forwards, and the game was on again. Then she retired to the other side of the floor and knelt down on one knee to get a good view of the action. Grace melted away, blushing with confusion.

"Grace Jones? Where's your partner?" shouted Hilda Schultz. "Oh, there she is. Let's get going. You two are still pretty clumsy on your jumps." Hilda was helping Grace and Grace's partner with the exercises on the big leather horse. Grace couldn't seem to get the hang of it. She spent the next ten minutes plunging at the horse, colliding with it, trying to vault neatly up on top of it, failing time after time. Once on top of the horse she was supposed to execute a series of tricks, gripping the handles with her hands, turning and twisting, swinging her legs around from one side to the other. But she had never yet managed to land on the horse in the first place. Trueblue Tom's muscle-building exercises hadn't helped her at all. Grace was strong and wiry, but her aim was bad and she didn't seem to know what to do with her arms and legs. If the Leader Corps requirements had included weight-lifting she would have been fine, but they called for timing and control, not just muscle.

Her partner wasn't any good at it either. She and Grace didn't even talk to each other. They just practiced and practiced, breathing hard, collapsing with *oooofs* and gasps, all angles and elbows, tangling on the mat, blundering into one another. Grace's partner was the famous Marjorie Zednick who was supposed to be such a genius. Marjorie wasn't in any of Grace's classes, so Grace had seen no evidence of her mental prowess. She certainly didn't look like a genius in the gym.

"You two don't have much coordination, do you?" said Hilda Schultz, shaking her head. "Here, watch Chatty Peak do it."

Chatty agreeably moved back into position behind the horse, took a lazy running jump, landed comfortably on top and then did a quick flip-flop that turned her completely around in the other direction.

"There. See that?" said Hilda. "Nothing to it. Now you two just practice awhile by yourselves."

"We'll never get in," said Marjorie Zednick gloomily.

This dire prediction brought tears to Grace's eyes. She *had* to get in. She tensed all her muscles and made another rush at the horse. This time she jumped too soon, coming down against the end of the horse, bruising her thighs against it, slipping backward and falling on her back on the mat. "*Ooooooooffff*," gasped Grace, gulping back the tears, struggling to her feet with Marjorie's hands under her elbows. Chatty's whistle was blowing again. Marjorie and Grace sat down on the bleachers, tired out.

"Are you Jewish?" said Marjorie.

"No," said Grace, rubbing her thighs, which were turning from their usual dead-white to purple and blue where they had been bruised. "Are you?"

"Yes," said Marjorie. Her face was gray with exhaustion, and there were blue shadows under her eyes. "We'll never pass," she said. "I wish I were athletic. I'd much rather be athletic than musical."

"Do you play the piano?" said Grace.

"Violin."

"Well, I play the piano, but I'm not musical. I'm not any good at that either."

"Come on," said Marjorie desperately. "Let's try again. We've got to get in. We've just got to."

The evening of the trials for the Girls Leader Corps came at the end of the first marking period. It was a disaster.

Grace's mother and father sat in the bleachers with the other parents and watched Grace blunder

and stumble, feeling more and more sorry for their daughter. Grace never did get up on the horse, although she lunged at it three times. All her basketball shots were wild. And there was a little dance she was supposed to do, arm in arm with Marjorie Zednick, while a victrola played "Turkey in the Straw." The two girls stepped all over each other, one of them hopping while the other was pointing her toe. Then poor Marjorie lost her balance and sat down with a thump. While she was struggling to get up, Grace shuffled her feet idiotically with a one-two, one-two, *hop*, one-two, because the music was still going *tiddle-iddle-iddle-iddle*, right past the place where they were supposed to join hands and circle round and round. At last Marjorie sprang up, threw herself frantically at Grace, grabbed her hands and pulled her around so hard that the two of them fell sprawling into Miss Bodecker, who was standing at one side, ticking off demerits. Miss Bodecker fell flat.

"Poor old Grace," said Grace's father to her mother, shaking his head with sympathy, as Grace and Marjorie shambled to their feet to stare in horror at the adored, revered Miss Bodecker, who seemed to have fainted dead away on the floor.

Miss Bodecker hadn't fainted really. She was only waiting for Mr. Chester to rush from the bleachers and help her up, which he promptly did, to her intense satisfaction. Then he hovered over her in romantic solicitude, and Miss Bodecker was really very grateful to Marjorie and Grace.

But they didn't know that, and they were miserable. Nor did Grace's mother and father know what to say to Grace as she hobbled with them out to the parking lot.

"Does it matter all that much?" said her father. "Will you really care if you don't get in?"

"I'll care," said Grace, feeling utterly wretched. This time she really had made a fool of herself in front of Chatty Peak. How could the two of them ever have anything in common, how could Grace ever reveal to Chatty Peak, as she did so often in her daydreams, her inmost secret self, her true self, the self she was making all alone, with absolutely no help from heredity or environment—if she were drummed out of the Girls Leader Corps before she even got in? And as for the uniform, the beautiful, beautiful uniform, was she never going to get to wear it? Not ever, after all?

Grace broke down altogether, and burst into tears.

Chapter 13

THE REWARDS
AND RESPONSIBILITIES
OF SUCCESS

But then the most amazing thing happened. Grace couldn't believe it. When the results of the tryouts for membership in the Girls Leader Corps were posted on the door of the gym the next day, lo, Grace Jones's name led all the rest. Well, it almost led all the rest. Marjorie Zednick's name was at the top.

Marjorie and Grace discovered this astonishing fact together, the first thing the next morning. Grace had taken the early trolley. Marjorie had played hookey from her eight o'clock violin lesson.

"But that's impossible," said Grace, a glow of happiness flowing over her. She looked at Marjorie and laughed. "It's just ridiculous."

Marjorie was grinning too. "I know. It's grades. Miss Bodecker told me they count your grades more than anything else. I got all A's."

"Oh, is that it?" said Grace. "Well, I got one D. I'm terrible in English. But all the rest were A's. I guess you're even more of a greasy grind than I am."

"No," said Marjorie. "I never get time to study. I have to practice all the time."

Grace felt humble in the presence of this genius who got all A's without ever cracking a book. "But why do you suppose they even bother to have those tryouts, if they don't even count?" Grace giggled. "We were so awful last night."

"I know," laughed Marjorie.

The two girls looked at the list again happily. "Look," said Grace, "we're supposed to report to the gym after school."

"To be measured for our uniforms, I'll bet," said Marjorie.

"Don't you just love them?" said Grace.

"I think they're the most beautiful uniforms in the whole world," said Marjorie.

Chatty Peak was there to welcome them in the gym after school, all the blessed ones who had been chosen to enter the pearly gates of the Girls Leader Corps. As the captain of the Leader Corps she gave them a brief pep talk. Then it was Miss Bodecker's turn to offer her warm welcome and sincere congratulations. "In conclusion," she said, "I only want to say, before we measure you for your uniforms"—all the girls looked at each other happily—"that those of us whose responsibility it is to be the leaders of the Girls Leader Corps are sure that you girls, chosen for your qualities of leadership and responsibility, will want to begin assuming that role immediately. I have checked your classroom schedules. You will find a list of your towel duties posted on the bulletin board. They are to begin at once."

Grace was puzzled. She raised her hand. "Towel duties, Miss Bodecker?"

"Chatty will explain," said Miss Bodecker. Then she picked up a bundle of hockey sticks and ran out of the gym to coach the girls' hockey team on the field.

Chatty stood up and put her hands on her hips. "Towel duty is passing out towels in the shower room for the girls' gym classes," she said.

"Oh, I see," said Grace.

Marjorie Zednick raised her hand. "Will we learn to referee?" she said, gazing admiringly at the silver whistle hanging around Chatty's neck.

Chatty fingered her whistle possessively. "Well, I don't know. I guess it's only the captain who does that."

After she had been measured for her uniform, Grace took a look at the schedule Miss Bodecker had posted on the bulletin board. There was hardly any need to look. She had only one study period every day, and that was now to be taken over by towel duty. Grace didn't mind. It meant she would have to carry more books back and forth to school, but that would develop her arm muscles, after all.

"I'll have to get my towel duty changed," murmured Marjorie. "My last period isn't really a study period. I go home early for a music lesson. I'll have to do my towel duty during lunch hour. Don't tell anybody. My mother would never let me do it. She thinks the Girls Leader Corps is a waste of time. She says it's just like the Hitler Youth."

"She does?" Grace was horrified. What sort of ghastly mother was that? "Do you have a music lesson every day?"

"Two. That's why I have to practice so much. I'm a child prodigy." Marjorie said it simply. She didn't seem to think it was anything special.

Towel duty turned out to be a damp job. The towel closet was right next to the girls' showers, and Grace soon discovered that she couldn't do her homework in there, because the steam made the ink on the pages of her notebook run. She couldn't even read, because the cloth covers of her books turned gummy in the moist air. All she could do was sit there in the dark, steamy room, which smelled of disinfectant and dirty socks, and slap down a clean towel on the counter for each hot, sweaty girl as she came by, and then take it back, soggy and wet, when the girl came out again.

Grace dutifully sat in the towel closet an hour every day all through the rest of October and then all through November. On the first of December everybody's schedule was changed around, and Grace found her place being taken by Marjorie Zednick at the end of the hour. Marjorie looked hungrily at a package of Tasty-Yeast that Grace had brought with her from the cafeteria.

"Here," said Grace. "Have some."

"Gee, thanks," said Marjorie. "I'm really starving."

Grace surrendered her place behind the counter and mopped her streaming hair with a clean towel, as Marjorie began slapping down more towels.

"Have you sold hot dogs at a football game yet for the Girls Leader Corps equipment fund?" said Marjorie.

"No," said Grace. "What's it like?"

"Cold," said Marjorie. "The wind really blows."

"Was it a good game? You get in free, don't you?"

"I didn't see it. The hot dog stand is over behind the bleachers. The wind really blows back there. The hot dogs freeze too."

"Oh," said Grace. If there was one thing she hated, it was being cold. But she would take her turn when the time came. And she knew Marjorie wasn't complaining either. They were dedicated, totally dedicated, both of them, to the service of the Girls Leader Corps.

Chapter 14

THE
HENRY TONJER
AFFAIR

Grace's friendship with Dot Moon had started on an uneasy footing, and it continued to have its ups and downs. One of the ups was at Christmastime, when they gave each other presents.

Each of them had tried hard to think in the other's language, in order to pick out something that would be just right, and there was much whispering and giggling and conferring with Sophie and Teenie. Grace's present for Dot was a pair of angora ankle socks. When Grace brought them over to the Moons' house on Christmas morning, Dot was delighted with them. She hugged Grace and tried on the socks right away. They fluffed out prettily over her ankles, making them look soft and puffy.

And Dot's present for Grace was even better. It was a real white cloth sailor's hat from the Army and Navy Store on King Street. Grace clapped the hat on the side of her head at once and shivered her timbers.

Dot laughed. "Did you see *Follow the Fleet*?" she said. "Ginger Rogers and Fred Astaire tap-danced all over the deck of a battleship in sailor suits. You look just like Ginger Rogers."

Grace beamed at her reflection in the mirror on Dot's dressing table. She did *not* look like Ginger Rogers; she looked more than ever like Trueblue Tom.

Christmas was one of the ups. But Valentine's Day was one of the downs. That was the day of the Henry Tonjer affair, and the friendship between Dot and Grace almost came apart at the seams.

Dot had a boyfriend now. It was Charley Blake. That was all right with Grace. *She* didn't care. The trouble was with Dot's second new boyfriend, Henry Tonjer. Grace wouldn't have cared about Henry Tonjer either, if he hadn't thought up such a hilarious way of hanging around Dot even when Charley was hanging around her too. Henry simply pretended to be Grace's boyfriend. The joke was that nobody could possibly think that Henry Tonjer would want the *tomboy* for a girlfriend, so it was all the more ludicrous when Henry fell on his knees beside Grace on February fourteenth, Valentine's Day, as she was getting her books out of her locker at the end of her last class. The corridor was crowded. Dot Moon and Charley Blake were there too, waiting for Grace.

"Be my valentine, Captain Bligh," pleaded Henry Tonjer in a loud voice, pressing his hand to his chest. "Allow me to carry your books to the trolley stop. I beg you on bended knee."

Grace stared at Henry Tonjer in horror, the blood rushing to her face. She caught on to the joke right away. "Oh, get up, you stupid—stupid—" she whispered furiously. She yanked on her coat, grabbed up her books, and started striding toward the door.

"Wait!" hollered Henry, chasing Grace down the hall on his knees, *thumpety-thumpety-thumpety-thump*, while Dot and Charley tittered, and everybody else caught on to the joke and laughed, Henry looked so ridiculous. "You know you like me, tomboy!" shouted Henry. "I'm irresistible! You can't deny it!"

"STOP it!" hissed Grace, turning around like an animal at bay. But she only succeeded in making the whole thing funnier than ever, because Henry pretended to be so dismayed he burst into loud sobs and hurled himself full-length on the floor.

"Oh, boo-hoo-hoo!" sobbed Henry.

Grace put her head down angrily, turned around again and charged at the door, but by the time she reached the sidewalk the four of them were marching along in some sort of order: Dot and Charley were walking together in front, looking back over

93

their shoulders and smirking, while Henry and Grace stumbled along in the back, struggling over Grace's books.

"Come on, now, Captain Bligh," said Henry, yanking at them with all his might, "you know you're too delicate and ladylike to carry all those great big heavy books, you poor little thing. Hey, Dot, I'll never smile again until you smile at me." (That was a song.)

Dot looked back at Henry and frowned as if she were mad at him, but Grace knew she was really enjoying having two boys flirting with her at the same time. Dot pretended to be shocked by the way Grace and Henry were wrestling all over the sidewalk. "Why, what's going on back there, you two?" she said.

"It's the tomboy," complained Henry, jerking and tugging at Grace's books. "She's trying to kiss me. Help me, Dot! Help me!"

Grace stamped her foot, her face blazing. "Oh, I am NOT."

"Why, Grace," simpered Dot, going along with the joke, "I'm surprised at you."

Charley Blake shook his head sorrowfully, grinning from ear to ear. "Shameful," he said, "I thought the pirate was Donald Waldorf's girlfriend. Fickle. Girls are so fickle. Look at that. Isn't that a shocking sight. She can't leave the poor boy alone."

When they climbed onto the trolley at last—Dot

gay and flattered, her face pink with praise, Grace a big gloomy girl with a glowering red face—they didn't know what to say to each other. Dot tried to make polite conversation, but Grace was so sore she didn't know what to say in return that wouldn't sound sulky and cross, so she didn't say anything.

Poor Trueblue Tom didn't have a clue to the proper behavior in this crisis, and neither did Captain Nancy or Captain John. Right now they seemed unreachable and far away and very small, like toy figures on a toy ship in a little glass bottle.

Chapter 15

GRACE'S
CORNER

It was at times like these that Grace needed a refuge, some peaceful and quiet spot where she could be by herself. The Valentine's Day disaster sent Grace straight home to her desk, her corner, her own private place on the back porch.

She had carved out her small empire around an old kitchen cabinet that had been wedged onto the porch behind the trash barrels and bundles of piled-up newspapers. The kitchen cabinet made a fine desk. There were cupboards and a flour bin over her head, and there were more cupboards under the porcelain counter. Since it had never been intended to be used as a desk, there was no room under the counter for her knees. She had to squeeze herself sideways with her neck craned over her shoulder.

But uncomfortable or not, it was nice back there. It was Grace's corner, her own place. It was where she kept her beautiful white paper and her lovely white envelopes and her long yellow pencils and her sweet-smelling paste and her pretty blue ink and her charming little boxes of tabs for sticking on the tops of things and her white reinforcements that looked like lifesavers and her shining gold stars. In the cupboard beside the flour bin lay her scrapbook of the British Royal Family, which she had put together in the old days when she had had delusions of grandeur. It embarrassed Grace to remember that she had once thought of herself as a secret princess, the future Queen of England, and she had long since given up collecting pictures of her ex-sisters, the Princesses Elizabeth and Margaret Rose.

Now she was keeping track of the war in Europe. Hitler had gobbled up Czechoslovakia and Poland, and England and France had declared war on Germany. Grace saved all the old *Life* magazines and cut out pictures of the German motorcycle corps, and photographs of Hitler making the Nazi salute, and she tore out the maps with their shifting, spreading, shaded areas showing the new territories of German control.

The whole thing was exciting in a horrible sort of way. Wouldn't it be horrible (but exciting) if the United States went to war? Grace knew that her father worried about it. He would turn grave at suppertime when the news was on the radio, and make everybody keep quiet, listening. The only other person who seemed to worry about the war was Dean Alexander. She had relatives and friends in Poland, and her faded eyes had been red with crying on the day Warsaw fell to the Germans.

Grace leafed through the latest discarded copy of *Life* and found a picture of Mussolini, the Italian dictator, making a speech from a balcony in Rome. She cut it out and pasted it into her scrapbook. Then she cleared away the magazine and the scrapbook and the scissors and paste, and brushed off the chipped porcelain counter in preparation for something much more important. Terribly important.

She had decided to write an epic poem. It would be long, like *The Ancient Mariner*, with dozens and dozens of verses. And it was going to be about God and the universe. This idea had occurred to Grace the night before. She had been lying in bed staring into the dark corner of her room, expecting, but not really expecting, but perhaps almost expecting to see Abou Ben Adhem's angel appear before her, a white and gold vision in the dark. And she had thought about God, and what it would be like to see him, too, there in the dark. And the first four lines of her poem had come to her quickly, easily, sliding into her head right out of the velvet dark.

Where is your blazing halo,
Your crown of raging fires?
The candlestick around your head
Of smoldering church spires?

Grace had been stunned by the perfection of these four lines. She had lain on her back memorizing them, saying them over and over, not sure where they had come from, fearful that they would slip back into nothingness and be gone forever. In the morning she had sat up, suddenly awake. Were they gone? Could she remember them? Yes, they were still there.

Now she was ready to write them down, and then she would go on with the rest of the epic poem. Grace took a sheet of white paper and made a sweeping W on it with her fountain pen. But the W turned into a blot. She threw the sheet of paper away and took a clean one. Then she wrote the four lines neatly and beautifully on the white page. Then she poised her pen over the paper again, waiting for inspiration, expecting a flood of verse to come rolling out, just the way it must have come rolling out for Samuel Taylor Coleridge.

Nothing happened. A blast of cold air hit the back of Grace's neck. She screeched, "Shut the door."

It was Teenie and Sophie. *Bang*, went the outside door. *Bang*, went the kitchen door.

Grace thought and thought. Nothing came. Oh, well, she couldn't expect inspiration to come along just any old time. She would have to wait for it patiently. She put the piece of paper away carefully in the drawer under the counter and bent down to the cupboard doors below the drawer for another project of hers, her paper-doll file.

It was a deep dark secret. Only Grace's mother and Sophie were in on it. Even Trueblue Tom carefully averted his eyes or politely went below deck whenever Grace took out her paper dolls. As for Captain Nancy and Captain John, Grace simply pulled down a sort of window shade in her mind and crouched behind it. Her paper dolls were a strictly private matter. No one else in the world must know, no jeering eyes must see. Teenie Moon's, for example. Grace looked over her shoulder and shifted her chair cautiously to hide what she was doing. How Teenie would laugh, if she knew!

And she would be right. There was no getting around it. Paper dolls were the sissiest thing any sissy silly stupid girl ever did. But Grace had built up a kind of complicated social structure around her paper dolls, a sort of whole little world, and she adored them.

The population of this little world lived in hundreds of envelopes in a filebox. Most of the paper dolls came from the funny-papers in the Sunday paper—Flash Gordon, Blondie Bumstead, Winnie

Winkle, Maggie Jiggs. The others came from furtive expeditions to the ten-cent store, where Grace would make sure nobody was looking, hastily pick out a folder of paper dolls, plunk down her dime on the counter, and then rush out with the paper dolls hidden in a plain paper bag.

She didn't bother to cut them out. She just folded the sheets and fitted them carefully into separate envelopes. And then the interesting part began. Take Alicia Van de Vere, for example. She was really Winnie Winkle, but Grace had so many Winnie Winkles she had given them different names. A forest of little index tabs covered with signs and symbols stuck up from Alicia's envelope. One of the symbols meant that she was married. Her husband was Flash Gordon, and he was folded into the same envelope. Another tab meant that they had a house of their own, a handsome Tudor mansion Grace had cut out of *American Home* magazine. There was a tab for their car, a luxurious Dusenberg, and another tab meant that Grace had worked out a whole family history for Winnie and Flash. They had met on a cruise ship bound for Rio de Janeiro. Flash had been the ship's captain, but poor Winnie had stowed away in the hold in order to rescue her father, who was tied up on the ship somewhere by kidnappers. Flash had discovered Winnie in her hiding place, fallen in love with her, rescued her father, retired from the sea, and moved with Winnie to Philadelphia, where he had become an investment banker. The last index tab on the top of the envelope indicated that a child had been born of this union. Flash and Winnie had a daughter (Shirley Temple), a lovable child who showed unmistakable signs of becoming an actress.

Many of the citizens of Grace's paper world were still homeless. She got up from her desk and pawed through the stack of newspapers until she found the rotogravure section of last Sunday's *Inquirer*. Somewhere inside it, she remembered, there was a picture of the elegant mansion and glass conservatory that belonged to Mr. and Mrs. Winslow S. DeForest. It would be just right for Maggie Jiggs. Grace found the picture and clipped it out. Then she sat down again, leaned back in her chair and studied the mansion dreamily. It was the home of the DeForest girls, it was their fairy-princess castle, their glittering pleasure-dome. In Grace's dream the DeForest girls were as beautiful as they were rich, and they drifted from room to room of the castle with flashing eyes and floating hair, feeding on honeydew at fragile gold tables beside the cascading shimmering fountain, drinking with delicate little sips the milk of paradise.

"Can I cut out a paper doll for you, Grace?" said Sophie, wandering out onto the back porch. Sophie loved Grace's paper dolls.

Grace jumped, and leaned over her desk to hide her filebox. Was Teenie coming too?

102

But Sophie was alone. "All right, Sophie," said Grace, with lordly good humor. "Why don't you cut out Flash Gordon and Winnie Winkle while I figure out what to do with all these Shirley Temples. I think I'll make this one a poor orphaned relative of Mr. and Mrs. Winslow S. DeForest. I'll have Mrs. DeForest fall into the Brandywine River and be carried away downstream. Then Shirley, who is the orphaned daughter of a logger in the Canadian Rockies, rescues her in a canoe. Mrs. DeForest adopts her and the butler teaches her to tap dance."

"Does she get in the movies?" said Sophie, fascinated as always by the glamorous lives of Grace's paper dolls.

"No, I think I'll have her become an airplane pilot. Where's Teenie?"

"She's down-cellar with Will."

"She is?" Grace looked up in alarm. Teenie was hanging around Will again. It seemed incredible to Grace, but her noble dignified brother didn't seem to mind. He was even learning Morse code with the help of Percy and Poncho. Grace had witnessed it. She had seen it with her own eyes only yesterday, down in the cellar where Will had his radio.

"Da-di-da-dit, da-da-di-da." That had been Percy, growling at Will from Teenie's lap.

"C something. I know—CQ." That was Will, leaning back in his chair with his eyes closed.

"Di-di-di-di-di-di-di-di-di-dit!" squealed Poncho.

He was being naughty.

"Now, stop it, Poncho," said Teenie, slapping his nose.

"Di-da-da, di-di-di-da-da, da-da-dit, di-da, di-di-da," squeaked Poncho, being good again.

Will was grinning with this eyes closed. "W3-GAU," he said. "That's somebody's call letters."

Grace simply couldn't *believe* it. Strong, sturdy, gruff, good old Will was firmly under the thumb of that arch-tyrant and little-girl demon, Teenie Moon. It was unnatural. It was horrible.

And now it was happening again. Well, this time Grace was going to put a stop to it. She jumped out of her chair and thumped down the cellar stairs.

There was Poncho, wearing Will's earphones, and there was Will, explaining to Percy how his super-heterodyne set worked.

"What's that thing there?" said Percy in his growly voice, pointing with one threadbare paw at a coil of wire sticking up out of the set.

"That's the antenna coupling coil," said Will.

" 'The antenna coupling coil,' Percy, *dear*, " corrected Teenie.

"Percy, dear," said Will, snickering.

"Kiss Poncho on the nose," commanded Teenie.

"*Smack*," went the obedient Will.

"In-cred-i-ble," breathed Grace out loud. Will looked around a little sheepishly, but then he picked up the other bear and kissed him loudly too.

Grace stamped upstairs again in utter disgust. What had happened to the world anyway? She stormed into the living room, plunked herself down at the piano and pretended to do her practicing, but really she was just making loud angry crashing chords.

Before long Teenie came upstairs and stuck her nose into the living room. "Good-bye, Grace Jones," she shouted above the din.

"So long," cried Grace, pounding on the piano till it shuddered with enormous discordant vibrations, *crashety-crashety-crash.*

"Say good-bye to—"

"*Good-bye,* Percy! *Good-bye,* Poncho!"

Teenie disappeared, and then the back door slammed. But a moment later Teenie was back, her brilliant blue eyes wide open, her face radiant with discovery. In one hand she held Flash Gordon, in the other Winnie Winkle. "You, a *sailor*, playing with paper *dolls*?" Teenie burst out laughing, and ran for the door again, a bear under each arm, a paper doll in each hand.

Grace was horrified. She had left her shameful playthings on her desk for anyone to see. She jumped up off the piano stool and bolted out the door after Teenie. "Give those back! I was just doing those for Sophie! Give them back!"

Teenie had a good headstart. But as Grace galloped out of the dark hollow behind the house and made the turn into the sunlit path beside the grape-vine, she came upon Winnie and Flash fluttering in the air over her head, turning end over end, soaring in little swooping flights like birds. Flash Gordon looked perfectly at home in his antigravity belt and floating cape. Grace plucked him neatly out of the air. But Winnie Winkle blew into a rhododendron bush and managed to land in a cold damp place on the ground. Grace dried her out on a towel and ironed her flat, but poor Winnie looked jaundiced and yellow ever after.

Chapter 16

DOWN THE HILL
WITH
TRUEBLUE TOM

With its paper dolls and its scrapbooks and its fragment of epic verse, Grace's corner was there on the back porch that winter waiting for her whenever she needed it—in time of trouble or on gray afternoons after school, or on sleety Saturdays and Sundays. But when spring came in earnest, when Grace's father stopped shoveling coal into the furnace, when wasps began knocking with glistening new wings around the windows of the house at noon on warm days, when green spears of narcissus began pushing up through the dead leaves around the front porch, Grace abandoned her desk and her scrapbook and her paper dolls and her poetry and flung herself out of doors. If Trueblue Tom felt in a crow's-nest kind of mood, she headed for her white pine tree. But there were pollywogs to snatch at in the lily pond, too, and there was all the rest of Mrs. Kane's tangled garden to explore. In the springtime, more than ever, it was the garden of Kubla Khan.

Kane, Khan! Grace had seen Mrs. Kane only once —a grim, faded old lady clinging to her teacups and her bric-a-brac, who didn't fit very well Grace's vision of the dashing Mongol emperor galloping with drawn scimitar through his forests and gardens and glittering caves of ice. But the dogwood flowering at the edge of the woods and the sprawling jungle of yellow forsythia beside the driveway and the somber grandeur of the great box hedges—these fitted the first part of the poem about Kubla Khan, and Grace herself, of course, had become the second. Beware, beware! Her flashing eyes, her floating hair!

One Saturday morning, after a wet week, the sky turned out to be a clear-washed blue. Grace hurried through her breakfast and headed for the garage. The grass would be too wet for walking, but the roads would be dry. She whistled for Whitey, trundled her brother's bicycle out of the garage, leaned it up against a tree, climbed on, and pushed herself away from the tree.

"Grace, Grace!" cried her mother from the kitchen window. "Be back by ten o'clock! You absolutely must not be late for your piano lesson. Not again. Not ever again. Those lessons cost—"

"One dollar, I know, I know," growled Grace between her teeth. "Okay," she called back over her shoulder, teetering along the dirt driveway, heading for River Road. Then she spent the next hour going around the four sides of a square.

The first side of the square was Bellefonte Hill, a long climb. Then Grace pedaled along the level street beside the trolley tracks all the way to Bellevue Road, and then she coasted down Bellevue to River Road, and breezed along River Road to the foot of Bellefonte Hill again.

The thrilling part was the plunge down Bellevue Road. Grace would sit back loosely on the seat, her short hair blowing backward, one arm hanging limp, her sleeves aflutter, and just let the bicycle drop, drop, drop down the hill, bounding over potholes, rattling and shaking, splashing through puddles, while Whitey raced after her on his short old legs, his tongue hanging out, his big eyes bulging.

It was a good time for Trueblue Tom and *The Ancient Mariner*. "Come on, Whitey," shouted Grace. The air rushed into her mouth, drying it out, blowing the words back in her throat. . . .

> *"God save thee, ancient Mariner,*
> *From the fiends, that plague thee thus!—*
> *Why look'st thou so?" "With my crossbow*
> *I* SHOT *the Albatross."*

Half of the thrill was the danger. Every single

time she flew down the hill Grace was afraid she would skid in the gritty dirt at the side of the road, or drive into a pothole, or not be able to slow down around the turn into River Road. She had taken some awful spills on Will's bike in the past.

Brake! Brake! This time she really was going too fast. The bike slowed down, wobbled on the uneven surface of the road, and skidded a little. Grace fell off into a puddle and skinned her knee and tore her middy and got all wet. She didn't care. Under the best of circumstances the only way she knew how to get off Will's bike was by falling off. The bar across the frame was so high her feet couldn't reach the ground. If she managed it just right, she could dismount by throwing out one leg and hurling herself away from the bike; then she'd keep her balance with a series of wild hops, while the bike coasted away and crashed to the ground on its side.

"Here, Whitey," called Grace, getting up. "Come on, Whitey. *Good* dog, Whitey."

Whitey came racing up, panting with exhaustion, his old face grinning with love, his massive chest heaving, his tightly curled tail wriggling. He put his front paws on her knees, and Grace hugged and petted him. Then she picked up the bike, leaned it against a telephone pole, climbed on, and pushed off from the pole. She wobbled precariously for a minute or two, then got going smoothly, making the turn onto River Road safely and easily, with Whitey trotting in the rear, her faithful companion and constant friend.

By the time she had gone around the square five times she had recited *The Ancient Mariner* twice through from start to finish in the teeth of the wind. Then she turned the handlebars of the bike sharply to the left into Mrs. Kane's driveway, and started on *Kubla Khan*.

> *In Xanadu did Kubla Khan*
> > *A stately pleasure-dome decree:*
> *Where Alph, the sacred river, ran*
> *Through caverns measureless to man*
> > *Down to a sunless sea.*
> *So twice five miles of fertile ground*
> > *With walls and towers were girdled round. . . .*

Come to think of it, decided Grace, hurling herself off the bike and guiding it on foot through the gap in the box hedge, that part of the poem sounded exactly like the DeForest place, with its long, forbidding wall. The DeForest girls floated before Grace's eyes again, those creatures of poetry and joy. She slogged along through the damp grass, pushing the bike down the hill through the rose garden, the briers tearing at her middy and her legs; and there in front of her Mrs. Winslow S. DeForest, too, came hazily to life, trailing her chiffon sleeves and veils and lace and perfume, bending down to smell the ghostly

112

colossal luxuriant cabbage roses. The roses were covered with glistening green Japanese beetles. A Japanese beetle crawled from one of the roses and climbed up on Mrs. DeForest's nose. Mrs. DeForest didn't seem to notice, and it clung there, horrible and bright, a diseased spot on her vague dreamy face.

Grace's mother had seen Mrs. DeForest once, and she was always talking about it. Mrs. Jones liked to pick up inexpensive secondhand clothes at the Salvation Army on King Street, and whenever she brought home a nice tweed suit or a peach satin evening gown she always said the same thing, "I'll bet it belonged to Mrs. DeForest. She brings her things to the Salvation Army, you know." And then Mrs. Jones would wear the things proudly, as if she were a kind of secondhand Mrs. DeForest. Grace suspected that the only reason her mother had chosen the music school on Harrison Street for Grace's piano lessons was because the DeForest girls went there too. She was probably hoping Grace would make friends with them. Well, there were no fairy princesses at the music school on the day Grace went to take her lesson. Her mother was out of luck.

Music school! Grace almost dropped the bicycle. Her piano lesson! She had forgotten it! She had forgotten it *again*! She was always late! Always! Her mother would be furious! Grace righted the bike and galloped it out of the rose garden, down through an overgrown privet hedge and into the gulley of

Chapter 17

THE
BIG BOX

The car jounced out of the driveway and whizzed down River Road. "Can't you do a little better than that, Grace?" said Mrs. Jones. "The edges. You haven't done the edges."

Grace worked on her forehead and her chin, feeling her rebellious spirits mount. The exhilarating morning had filled her with a giddy spirit of True-blue Tomism, and this morning he was more swashbuckling than ever; in fact, for once, he felt more like a pirate than the first mate of *The Flying Cloud*.

"Your knees, Grace. Can't you do something about those knees? And take off that dreadful middy."

"I can't," said Grace, "unless you want me to take my piano lesson in my petticoat."

"Oh, *Grace*."

At the Harrison Street Music School Mrs. Jones zoomed the car up to the curb, spilled Grace out and watched her gallop up the stone steps. Then she drove off, shaking her head. Grace was still reciting *The Ancient Mariner*—

> *Water, water, everywhere,*
> *And all the boards did shrink;*
> *Water, water, everywhere,*
> *Nor any drop to drink.*

As she flung the door open she was proclaiming the next verse at the top of her lungs (it was her tiptop favorite verse in the whole poem)—

> *The very deep did rot: O Christ!*
> *That ever this should be!*
> *Yea, slimy things did crawl with legs*
> *Upon the slimy sea.*

There were two girls waiting in the front hall. They looked up, startled, at the apparition silhouetted in the doorway, then flinched and shrank backward. Grace didn't know their real names, but she had seen them before, and she thought of them as the Pug sisters, because they had fat little pug faces and pink chubby cheeks and pudgy fat legs in woolly stockings and short yellow hair like fat little Dutch boys. Now they looked as if their hair wanted to stand up on end with fright.

"Oh, there you are, Grace," said Mrs. Robinson, Grace's piano teacher, hurrying out into the hall. "Come on in, you're late."

Half an hour later Mrs. Robinson dismissed Grace, then stuck her head into the next room to confide in her fellow-teacher, Mr. Angelo, who had just dismissed one of the Pugs. "I don't know why that child's parents waste their money on lessons," she said. "She hasn't got a speck of talent. And they obviously don't have any money to spare, from the looks of her."

"The ways of parents are inscrutable," sighed Mr. Angelo.

Her lesson had gone badly, but Grace didn't care, now that it was over. In the front hall she found the two Pugs once again, pulling on their woolly coats. Heartlessly, Trueblue Tom fired another broadside. "BEWARE!" thundered Tom, glaring at the bigger of the two Pugs. "BEWARE! BEWARE! My flashing eyes! My floating hair!"

Both Pugs turned pale and jerked backward. Grace threw herself out the door and took the steps three at a time, shouting, "Shiver my timbers!" and "Jibbooms and bobstays!" like Captain Nancy. She would have liked to jump into her mother's DeSoto and set sail at once, skimming briskly away from the dock, busy with the sails and shrouds, shouting more verses from *The Ancient Mariner* or singing "Blow the Man Down."

But her mother was late. Grace wearied of being dramatic, and sat down patiently on the stone wall to wait. But the first car that came along was for the Pugs, not for Grace.

The car was plain but highly polished. The chauffeur wore a plain brown uniform. Mrs. Pug sat in the back seat. Grace had seen her before. She was plump and wholesome-looking, like her daughters. Today she met Grace's eye, and then to Grace's astonishment she put her hand out the window and kinked her finger at Grace.

Obediently, Grace hopped down from the stone wall and bent down beside the car to look in at Mrs. Pug, while the two Pug sisters hurried behind the car, away from mad, insane Grace.

"Here, dear," said Mrs. Pug to Grace, "this is for you." She was grappling with an enormous box, poking it through the window at Grace. The box was wrapped in brown paper and tied with a string. It was as big as a coffin.

"For me?" said Grace, pointing at her chest in disbelief.

"Yes, of course. A gift for you and your family." Mrs. Pug was nodding and smiling graciously. Her two daughters were pale, dim, staring spots of white beside her in the dark interior of the car.

118

Grace took hold of the end of the big box and dragged it awkwardly out of the window. "Thank you," she said.

"Just pull it away from the car, dear," said Mrs. Pug.

"Oh, sorry," said Grace. She dragged the box away from the car. The chauffeur revved the engine. Mrs. Pug nodded in a queenly way at Grace, her daughters stared at Grace wanly, and the car disappeared smoothly around the corner.

Grace's mother was just driving up. She pulled to a stop and beamed at Grace. "I told you the DeForests come here," she said, leaning across the front seat, opening the car door. "That was Mrs. Winslow S. DeForest who just drove away." Then Mrs. Jones saw the big box. "What's that?" she said sharply, as Grace began struggling it into the car.

"It's a box," said Grace. "But—do you mean those *Pugs* are the DeForest girls?" She was flabbergasted. Why, they were just fat little girls, not creatures of poetry and joy at all, not fairy princesses, not damsels with dulcimers from the poem about Kubla Khan.

But Mrs. Jones wasn't listening. She was looking at the big box suspiciously. "Where did you get it?" she said.

"*She* gave it to me. Mrs. DeForest. Just now."

"What's in it?"

"I don't know."

120

Mrs. Jones's face flushed a dark red. "It *couldn't* be—she *wouldn't*—"

But it was. She had. When the big box was unwrapped and opened up on the kitchen floor, it was bulging with secondhand clothes, with bristly coats too small for the DeForest sisters, with dresses Mrs. Winslow S. DeForest had worn to social events which Mrs. Jones had read about in the rotogravure, with suits that had once belonged to the illustrious Mr. Winslow S. DeForest himself.

"I thought so," said Mrs. Jones bitterly. She picked up the topmost dress by the tips of her fingers and dropped it disdainfully in a heap.

"It's just like the other one," said Grace.

"What other one?"

"The dress you have upstairs. You know, from the Salvation Army. Only that one's peach-color and this one is blue. Now you have two." Grace rummaged in the box and pulled out a tweed coat. It looked warm and light, just like the ones the Pugs had been wearing today. Grace started to try it on.

Her mother was staring at her. Then suddenly she reached out and slapped Grace's hand hard. "You put that right back," she said. Then she burst into tears. Grace was horrified. She put the coat back in the box and, silent and dismayed, helped her mother tuck everything in the box neatly and wrap it up again with the same paper and string.

The big box went back to Mrs. DeForest that very

121

afternoon. Grace's mother mailed it from the post office across the city square from the DeForest Building. The postage was four dollars. Attached to the outside of the package was a stiff white envelope sealed with a blob of gold sealing wax on which Grace's mother had stamped a fancy letter J.

Grace didn't know what her mother had written on the stiff white notepaper inside the envelope, but she thought a lot about the haughty things *she* would have said, if *she* had been writing the letter—

My dear Mrs. DeForest,

   How sad that you did not know that my daughter Grace is the future Queen of England! May I suggest that you give these things to The New England Home for Little Wanderers? It is the favorite charity of our butler.

                    Yours regretfully,
                    Louise Camberwell Jones

Or, better still—

My dear Mrs. DeForest,

   I regret to say that we cannot assist you financially at this time by buying any of the clothing you submitted for our inspection, since we purchase our entire wardrobe in Paris, France. However I hope you will accept the small gift of one dollar ($1) enclosed herewith.

                    In deepest sympathy,
                    Louise Camberwell Jones

122

After that Grace had her piano lessons at home, right in her own living room, with a new teacher, an old lady named Mrs. Flagg. Mrs. Flagg always began each lesson the same way. "The piano," she would say, "is the king of instruments. Never forget that, dearie." Mrs. Flagg only knew how to play a few pieces herself, like "The Happy Farmer" and "Moonlight on the Hudson," but she only charged a quarter.

After Grace had pounded the stuffing out of "The Happy Farmer," Mrs. Flagg demonstrated "Moonlight on the Hudson," her long blood-red, talon-like fingernails clicking feebly on the keys, making vague dabs at the chords with the left hand and sloppy tiddling trills with the right.

Mrs. Flagg wasn't fussy and demanding like Mrs. Robinson at the Harrison Street Music School. She just sat behind Grace in an armchair taking naps while Grace did her scales. Whenever the noise from the piano stopped she would wake up with a little snort. "That's very nice, dear," she would say. "The piano is the king of instruments. Never forget that."

Chapter 18

DOLLAR
DAY

A quarter for piano lessons—that was the sort of bargain Grace's mother liked. She was a whiz at discovering sales and auctions, and she knew where to find secondhand stores like the Salvation Army, and she was always going off shopping and coming back with the DeSoto full of slightly chipped plates or dusty carpets with holes in the middle or old dressers with broken mirrors she had got for fifty cents.

Her mother was clever, Grace knew that. She could make a loaf of bread, or wire a lamp, or upholster a chair. She could even repair the roof, or putty a window, or fix the washing machine. She could change a flat tire. She never needed to hire anybody to fix anything because she could fix it herself. Her hands were always green with dye or white with paint or scratched from repairing a screen door.

You couldn't help but admire her cleverness and energy. Grace's father would shake his head when he saw the latest broken wreck his wife had dragged home, but then he would be as amazed as the rest of them when she transformed it into a fresh new cupboard for dishes, or a record cabinet, or a pair of bedside tables. "One of these days I'm going to buy you a mink coat with the money you save, Louise," he would say.

But Grace and Sophie sometimes wished their mother were not quite so thrifty, because for them it meant the difference between good clothes from Braunstein's and cheap clothes from Dixie Brothers Dry, and that was a big difference. Braunstein's was in the fashionable part of Market Street, way up near the DeForest Building and the library. It was hushed and quiet and expensive in there, with glittering glass display cases and carpets on the floor. Dot Moon's mother often went there, and the women behind the counters would poke their smooth manicured hands into the spidery stockings to show Mrs. Moon how gauzy and thin the silk was.

But Grace's mother never went to Braunstein's. She liked the tumble and shove of Dixie Brothers Dry Goods Store, and the cheap prices and the sales. So Grace and Sophie and Will were dressed from head to foot in Dollar Day specials from Dixie Brothers Dry. And their clothes were sleazy, there was no getting away from it. After all the sizing and starch came out in the wash, their new clothes always looked a little limp and out of shape.

There was to be another Dollar Day on the Saturday after the episode of the big box. That Friday evening Mrs. Jones took her daughter aside. There was a look on her face that meant she was going to say something important.

"Grace," said Mrs. Jones, "tomorrow is Dollar Day."

"I know," said Grace.

"I think it's time you learned how to handle money. So I want you to go shopping for some new school clothes all by yourself tomorrow. I think ten dollars would be about right."

Grace saw through her mother's little scheme. Mrs. Jones had been complaining about Grace's middy all year long, and about her sneakers and so on, and now she was hoping that if Grace were to choose some new clothes for herself she might want to show them off, she might really *wear* them, and put away her middy. Well, of course Grace would never do that, but it would be fun to spend ten dollars.

"Would you like that, Grace?"

"Oh, yes."

So the next morning Mrs. Jones and Grace and Sophie all drove into town together to take advantage of Dollar Day. They stood in a tight three-person huddle in the front entrance of Dixie Brothers Dry Goods Store, stemming the urgent riptide of bargain-hunting lady shoppers, and Mrs. Jones counted out ten one-dollar bills into Grace's hand.

"Do I have to spend it all in Dixie Brothers Dry?" said Grace, shouting to make herself heard above the din.

"Why, no, I guess not," Mrs. Jones shouted back. "It's Dollar Day all over town. But of course Dixie Brothers has the best buys. Now you will be sensible, won't you, dear? Ten dollars is a lot of money for one young lady to spend all at once."

"Oh, yes. Yes, I will."

"Well, then, meet us right here at noon. Come on, Sophie!" cried Mrs. Jones. "Follow me and hang on tight!"

Grace watched her mother and her little sister plunge into the crowd of women who were surging eagerly around the big wooden bins full of rayon stockings and panties and cotton aprons and house-dresses. Then she turned away and headed straight up the street for Braunstein's. Whatever she spent her ten dollars on, it wasn't going to be something sleazy and cheap from Dixie Brothers Dry. It was going to be the best there was to be had, the very best.

The shoppers in Braunstein's were better dressed than the ladies in Dixie Brothers Dry, but they were just as greedy and determined. They crowded into the perfumed air of the store, their feet sinking deep into the carpet, their eyes darting this way and that to see if there were any cashmere sweaters marked down, or camel's-hair coats, or gossamer stockings. Grace looked too. She looked at everything. She squeezed between the ladies. She studied the prices. She read the labels. But she couldn't seem to make up her mind. How could she know whether something was the very best of its kind or not? If it was marked down, didn't that mean there was something wrong with it?

Squeezing her way out of the store again, Grace ambled back down the street in the direction of Dixie Brothers Dry, glancing idly at the store windows as she went by. Whatever she bought that morning, it had to be like twenty-four carat gold, the very best of its kind, the farthest thing from being marked down. Unique! One-of-a-kind! Something that would last forever. Grace's hand in her pocket felt hot, clutching the folded dollar bills. Somehow that dirty Dollar Day money had to be transformed into something wonderful and beautiful, something to keep forever.

By this time Grace was floating high above the greedy pushing and pawing of Dollar Day. She felt sorry for the women hurrying past her, their faces hungry for shopworn merchandise. *She* would not be like that. She would buy something precious, something beautiful ("a miracle of rare device"!)— not at Braunstein's, not at Kennard's, not at Woolworth's, not at Grant's, not at the Rexall Drug Store, not at—

Then Grace's floating feet came down to earth. The next store was Plummer's, the silver and jewelry shop. There was no big Dollar Day sign in the window. Plummer's was above such low commercial practices.

Grace caught herself thinking, as she opened the door, that the DeForests must come to Plummer's whenever they wanted any silver or jewelry (or crystal goblets, in case either of those fat little girls wanted to drink the milk of paradise).

And it was at Plummer's that Grace found what she wanted. "I'll take that one," she said, peering into the glass case, pointing at a gold locket.

It was the smallest one they had, but it was also the most expensive, because it was solid twenty-four carat gold. It was the best.

On the way back to Dixie Brothers Dry Goods Store, Grace ran into Dot and Teenie Moon. They had been to the Dollar Day sale at Braunstein's. Proudly Grace opened her precious little package and displayed her prize.

"Why, Grace," gushed Dot, "you're in love."

That again! "I am not," said Grace in hot denial.

"Henry Tonjer?" suggested Teenie in a cheery shout. "Donald Waldorf? Grace is going to put Donald Waldorf's picture in her locket and wear it next to her heart."

"Oh, stop it," said Grace. "I have to meet my mother now. Good-bye." She stuffed her locket back in the bag and hurried away to Dixie Brothers Dry, worrying about what her mother would say when she saw how the ten dollars had been spent. She wouldn't like it, decided Grace. She wouldn't like it at all.

Grace was right. Her mother was dismayed. Her good idea for improving Grace's appearance hadn't worked at all. But then she laughed, and she didn't scold Grace. (But it would be a long time before she tried *that* trick again.)

When they got home from their morning of shopping, Sophie ran to try on her new school dress and patent-leather shoes, and Grace began looking around on her kitchen-cabinet desk for the latest issue of the school paper. She wasn't in love with Henry Tonjer or Donald Waldorf, but it did seem a waste to have a locket and not put anybody's picture in it. Carefully she snipped out a tiny face from a photograph of the school orchestra, and wedged it into the infinitesimal gold frame inside the locket. It was a picture of Mr. Chester. Trueblue Tom might sneer at sissy things like boyfriends and crushes and falling in love, but, Tom or no Tom, Grace had to admit to a slight weakness for Mr. Chester. She didn't spend much time thinking about it. Mr. Chester was as far away from Grace as Clark Gable was from Dot Moon.

She strung the locket on a ribbon, tied it around her neck, and showed it to her brother Will. (Only the outside, of course, not the inside.)

Will shook his head. "I call that a waste of money," he said.

But it wasn't a waste of money for Grace. It was twenty-four carat gold. It would last forever. It was the best there was.

Chapter 19

THE RING

There was something else that was gold, something else that would last forever. It was the ring. The ring hung over Grace's class at the Winslow S. DeForest School all that year, golden and glittering, mysterious and unattainable.

Actually, of course, there were two rings. The American Legion was going to award two gold rings at the end of the year, one to the Best All-around Boy, the other to the Best All-around Girl.

When Grace's father heard about it, he clapped Grace on the back. "You'll be it, I'll bet," he said.

"No, no," said Grace. "It's not like that. You don't understand."

"Well, what is it like then?"

"Well, it's not just for being a greasy grind."

"A greasy grind?"

"You know, doing your homework, and getting A's."

"I'll bet I know what it is," joked Mr. Jones. "They give the ring for the Best All-around Girl to the fattest girl in the class, the one who's biggest all-the-way-around. You'll never get it, after all. You're too skinny."

"Ruth Marshall," giggled Grace. "They'll give it to Ruth Marshall. She's simply huge."

But joking aside, Grace thought she knew what it was that won the ring. It was being *like* the ring, golden and glittering. It was being the kind of person who heard her name echoing up and down the hall between classes. It was Milly Lee and Daniel Margolis walking down the hall together. It was, "Hiya, Milly. Hello, Daniel." . . . "Milly, Milly, Milly." . . . "You look darling today, Milly." . . . "Attaboy, Dan." . . . "Say, boy, Dan."

The ring floated over the class, hovering now over this head like a sort of halo, now over that, then drifting away to hold itself aloof as if it were waiting for a worthier brow.

Grace often looked at herself in the mirror over her mother's dressing table to see if there was the faintest aura of gold about her own person. She made checklists again, staring at herself, studying her face and her hair and her clothes and the contents of her mind to see how her OUTSIDE and INSIDE were faring. On the first day of spring her checklist went like this:

OUTSIDE

Item: Girl, Grace P. Jones by name—and, hey! she was taller! All of a sudden. It had happened overnight. And bigger! She was bigger all over. Her skirt looked about a foot too short. Her middy was still plenty big, but she had left that at school, and her blouse was much too tight. Those Dixie Brothers bargains always shrank a little, but this was ridiculous. (Check.)

Item: Brown hair—too long! If she were going to be loyal to Trueblue Tom she would have to snip off an inch or two here and there. (Check? No, wait a minute.)

Grace stared at her reflection intently, then shook her head to make her hair float from side to side. It floated beautifully. Well, on second thought, maybe she wouldn't cut it for awhile yet, after all. (Check? Check.) Now for the rest of her:

INSIDE

Item: Well, of course the inside was Tom, trueblue as always, first mate of *The Flying Cloud*, under the command of Captains Nancy and John, et cetera, et cetera. (Check.)

134

But was there a glamorous glitter of gold about Grace Perkins Jones? Either inside or outside? Alas, no, decided Grace. And without any glitter of gold she would never win the ring. The teachers were going to be the judges and that was what they fell for.

Just look at the way Dean Alexander was about Daniel. The old lady was crazy about him, anybody could see that. He would come shuffling into Latin class ten minutes late, and Dean Alexander would glare at him with her faded eyes. But then she would pick out the easiest Latin phrases for him to translate, because she knew perfectly well he hadn't done his homework, and she hated to show him up.

"*Puellae sunt pulchrae,*" was the kind of easy bit she saved for Daniel. Everybody else in the class knew it meant "girls are pretty." But not Daniel. "That's—ah—*teachers* are pretty?" hazarded Daniel. This was a shot in the dark, a wild outrageous compliment for old Dean Alexander.

"No, no, Daniel," muttered Dean Alexander, trying hard not to show that she liked it. "You should know by now that *puella* means girl. Let's try something else. Try conjugating the verb 'to be.'"

So that was Daniel. He couldn't help being gold, even in Latin class. But it was on the basketball court that he really shone.

Grace went to the last big interscholastic game of the year and sat in the bleachers with the other members of the Girls Leader Corps. Even Marjorie Zednick was there, although Grace knew Marjorie was supposed to be at home taking a violin lesson. She was there for the same reason Grace was there. The new Leader Corps members were wearing their uniforms in public, and that was still a special kind of thrill. Grace and Marjorie sat side by side, admiring each other's crisp white blouses and black basketball shoes, enjoying the way the stiff pleats of their tunics lay in graceful folds over their black stockings. Ever since Grace had put on her uniform for the first time, she had hoped to strike up a friendship at last with Chatty Peak, because now she really felt like a comrade-in-arms, a blood brother, a colleague, a genuine fellow member of Chatty's Leader Corps.

But the opportunity never came. The friendship hadn't happened yet. And today Chatty had something much more important to do than sit in the bleachers with the rest of the Leader Corps. She was kneeling on the sidelines with a towel over her shoulders, just like the boys who were waiting their turn to play. Every now and then she would shout through a megaphone at Daniel Margolis as the game surged past her. "Attaboy, Daniel!" . . . "You can do it, Daniel!" . . . "Sink it, Daniel!"

You couldn't blame her, decided Grace. Daniel Margolis was always smack in the middle of the racing and lunging boys, running forward with his long-legged lope, his huge hands and feet working

smoothly, his hair falling in damp brown locks over his forehead, a big grin on his face as if he were enjoying his own swiftness and easy grace. Effortlessly he sank basket after basket. Compared to Daniel all the other boys on the floor were wiry bundles of perspiration, even Donald Waldorf. They were just nervous shadowy blobs with skinny white legs, and all of them were out of focus anyway, because everyone in the gym had eyes only for Daniel Margolis. He moved in a gold mist that clung to him like sweat.

And then in the last few minutes of the game Chatty had her chance. The basketball coach let her be the referee. Instantly Chatty was all over the court, dodging in and out, blowing her whistle furiously for a foul, tossing the ball to Daniel for the free throws. It was odd, thought Grace, the way Daniel never seemed to notice Chatty Peak. It was almost as if she weren't there at all. He just didn't seem to see her. You would think the two top athletes in the school would be boyfriend and girlfriend. But Daniel already had a girlfriend, Milly Lee, the angora-sweater girl.

And Milly was gold, too. They were both gold. Gold like the two gold rings.

Chapter 20

THE SHADOW
OF THE
DOME OF PLEASURE

The Henry Tonjer affair had opened a gulf between Grace Jones and Dot Moon. But the gulf didn't last. Dot was too generous and good-hearted. Grace couldn't be mad at her for long. Especially after the way Dot stuck up for Grace on the first day of school after spring vacation. When that day was over Grace was no longer the only girl who had come to blows in the Winslow S. DeForest School. Dot Moon, too, had put up a fight, and it was a fight on Grace's behalf, a fight with Ruth Marshall of all people, Ruth Marshall the mammoth girl.

Dot and Grace had been walking together down the hall one morning when Ruth Marshall, wallowing closer and closer from the other direction, had started jeering. "Hey, Dot," she had said loudly so that everyone in that end of the building could hear, "is that your boyfriend? Pretty funny-looking boy-friend, if you ask me."

And Dot had kicked her. To Grace's astonishment Dot Moon had flown at Ruth Marshall and kicked her in the colossal calf of her enormous right leg, like a flea attacking a hippopotamus. Ruth had squealed and slapped Dot on the left cheek. Her hand was pudgily small, but behind it was the weight of an arm like a side of beef. Puny little Dot had been bowled right over.

Then Grace got into it, of course, charging in with pummeling fists, shouting, "You big bully." But suddenly Dean Alexander was there in front of her. "That will be enough of that," she had said quietly, and in a moment she had swept Grace and Dot into Mr. Stanley's room and hurried Ruth off to her study hall.

"She just made me so *mad*," whispered Dot, sitting down next to Grace, rubbing her sore cheek.

"Wow, Dot," said Grace, "that was really something. You were really brave."

So the two of them kept on being best friends. And by the time Dot's birthday came along in April it was no surprise that she shared it with Grace Jones. Dot's big birthday present was money to buy new clothes with. But instead of buying clothes she decided to spend her money on four tickets to the movies, a grand opening, the first day of a big new picture at Loew's, the most expensive movie theater

140

in Swedesville. And the movie was famous already. It had cost millions and millions of dollars. It was *Gone with the Wind*. The four tickets were for Dot and Grace and Teenie and Sophie. *Gone with the Wind*. At Loew's.

"Don't you think the movie will be awfully long for Sophie?" said Mrs. Jones doubtfully.

"Oh, no. Oh, please," begged Sophie. So her mother let her go.

The big day turned out to be raw and cold. When the four girls got off the trolley they had to crowd in at the end of a long line of people, all waiting to buy tickets to *Gone with the Wind*. Dot and Grace and Teenie and Sophie didn't mind that. Their only fear was, what if they didn't get in? Their coats were all too thin, except for Grace's, which was just a jacket over her father's Navy middy. On warm days Grace nearly cooked in her middy, but today it was a solid blanket of blue serge comfort. The four girls huddled together, jigging up and down on their cold feet, giggling with anticipation. The other people in the line were happy too, and they made jokes about Scarlett O'Hara and Rhett Butler. Slowly they shuffled ahead in the line, little by little, leaning forward with eagerness.

After half an hour the marquee was very near. It hung way out over the pavement, casting a glamorous yellow shadow on the people underneath, because it was made of great projecting rays of yellow glass. Above it the name of the theater sparkled in electric bulbs . . .

L
O
E
W
S

It felt wonderful to be crowding closer and closer to that splendid marquee and that glowing luminous brilliant radiant name. Now the four girls could see the ticket person in the lighted glass box who had the power of life and death over everyone in the line. She was a beautiful doll with platinum hair, a part of Hollywood, almost a starlet herself, a kind of preview of the glamorous wonders to come. The ticket girl didn't look at the humble supplicants who pushed their money at her through the opening in the glass. Nor did she give any hint of how many more of the shivering people in the line would get in to see the picture and how many would be rebuffed and sent back into the drab streets and the drab trolleys and their own drab lives again. She didn't care who got in and who didn't. Only once did

she look up from the busy *slap*, *slap* of her plump manicured fingers, and that was when a colored man and his girlfriend walked past the waiting line of people and paused to look at the posters of the stars of *Gone with the Wind* beside the ticket window. The girl in the lighted box rapped sharply on the glass and shook her head at them. They couldn't come to Loew's, that was what she meant. The man and the girl looked at the doll in the glass box with their speaking dark eyes, then turned and strolled on again. Grace turned and watched them go. They hadn't meant anything, she thought angrily. They were just looking. They knew they couldn't come in. The colored people had their own theater down on King Street. But Grace knew that it would be a long time before *Gone with the Wind* came to King Street.

The glass box was very near. "Here, Grace," commanded Dot. "You buy the tickets if I'm not back in time." She thrust her dollar bills at Grace, then hurried away around the corner. In a few minutes she was back. Generous noble Dot, Dot the Provider, had rushed across the street to Liggett's Drug Store and the delicatessen, and now she was back with a paper bag of dill pickles and another one of candy. "I was going to get Baby Ruths and Mounds, but then I thought, gosh, four hours. So I got Walnettos instead, they take so long to chew." She was just in time to push her money through the hole in the glass

144

box. Four hearts beat as one with fear and hope. The girl swept up the money, tore off four tickets, and slapped them down with the same gesture she had been using all afternoon. They were in!

The morning show was over. People were beginning to pour out, stumbling over their clumsy feet, their faces pale and blinking. Some of the women's faces were streaked with tears.

"How was it?" said Teenie, boldly addressing a woman who was wiping her eyes on her coatsleeve.

"Just marvelous," said the woman.

"Here we go," said Sophie excitedly. A young man in a blue uniform, his hair combed back in a pompadour, was unfastening the velvet rope, and now the waiting crowd was surging forward. Other uniformed young men were leading them down the black aisles of the theater, guiding their footsteps with flashlights, moving backward as if the customers were royalty. They really gave you your money's worth at Loew's.

The seats were thick soft plush. Grace and Dot and Sophie and Teenie sank into them, grinning at each other happily in the dark. The paper bags rustled and passed from hand to hand. "Have a bite of my pickle?" said Dot, generously, nobly.

"Oooh, no," said Grace, "not after a Walnetto. Thanks anyway."

"It's starting," whispered Teenie. "*Ssssh, ssssh.*"

The lights were dimming. The vast music that

accompanied the introduction to the movie began sweeping through the theater, and the vast title, GONE WITH THE WIND, pulsed at them on the screen. A sense of being part of this vastness filled Dot and Grace and Teenie and Sophie and everyone else in the theater, and they all leaned back enraptured, drinking it all in.

There before them was Tara, the southern mansion that belonged to Vivian Leigh, who played Scarlett O'Hara. And there was Scarlett, clinging to a bedpost while her black mammy tugged at her corset strings.

"I hate her, don't you?" confided Teenie, nudging Grace.

"Poor Rhett Butler," agreed Grace. Scarlett was mean to all the men she fell in love with.

"Have another Walnetto?" said Dot, leaning across the screen.

Four hours. The movie was going to last four hours.

Chapter 21

THE EVER-SO-BOUNDING MAIN

Then Grace had a birthday too, in the middle of the month of May. But she didn't share it with Dot Moon, or with anybody else but her father, because her present was so special, so personal, so private, so glorious.

Her father was going to teach Grace to sail. At last it was no longer an idle promise. He was going to rent a little catboat just as soon as the boatyard at Rehoboth Beach opened up for the season, and then every Saturday morning he was going to give Grace lessons in sailing. At last Grace Jones was going to set foot on a swaying deck, she was going to begin her life on the bounding main, and she was over-joyed. Poor Trueblue Tom had been feeling a little faint and transparent lately, but now he zoomed back into good health and snapped to attention.

Captain Nancy beamed her approval. So did Captain John. Grace brought her sailor middy home from school, and when the great day dawned she put on the woolen middy and her sailor hat and swaggered around, even though the sun had come up bright and red, promising hot weather.

"Have a good time, Grace dear," said her mother, waving good-bye.

"A good time?" said her father. "Don't worry. Rapture and ecstasy will be the order of the day."

Grace fell in love with the catboat at once. It was a right little, tight little craft with a single sail. Sweltering in her hot middy she strolled along the edge of the dock, glorying in the feeling of being part of a chapter in one of Arthur Ransome's books. John's and Nancy's world had come to life, and she was smack in the middle of it at last. She began tossing out nautical remarks to impress the boy who was taking her father's money. "I see she's gaff-rigged. Does she ship much water? Do you want me forward or aft? Shall I take the tiller?"

"Wait till we get past the breakwater," said her father. "Then you can take over. I'll show you what to do. Here, I'll get in first and help you aboard."

Mr. Jones stepped cautiously off the dock into the boat, and crouched down on the stern thwart. Then he reached up for Grace's hand. Scorning his assistance, Grace stepped down heavily and started to stalk forward like Captain Ahab in *Moby Dick*.

"Grace! Sit down!" shouted her father, as the little boat plunged and rocked. Grace threw out her arms and fell sprawling. And then the excitement and the heat and the rolling of the boat and the shame all boiled up inside her. She leaned over the side and threw up. The boy on the dock snickered.

Mr. Jones leaned forward and patted Grace on the back. "Poor old girl. Are you all right now?"

Grace groaned and sat up, gray with shock. "I guess so," she said, clinging to the side with both hands.

"It happens to the best of us," comforted her father. "Just duck down a minute while I come about." He shoved the tiller over, the bow swerved, the sail flopped over Grace's head, and the little boat began moving forward, bobbing across the small waves lapping around the dock, its sail rippling. Mr. Jones pulled the rope tighter. The sail stopped flapping and the catboat moved forward with a sprightly motion, the water creaming in tiny bubbles around its bow.

Grace perked up. They were making their way smoothly through a cluster of motorboats and sailboats anchored within the breakwater. By the time her father was ready to come about for the third time, Grace was handling the tiller herself, shoving it over smartly and leaning on it as the little boat nosed in the other direction. Her heart began to swell with pride. Soon they would be on the other side of the breakwater and out on the open sea—one brave little ship—alone, alone, all, all alone, alone on a wide, wide sea! "Blow the man down, bullies," sang Grace happily, "blow the man down! Way, hey, blow the man down!"

"Watch out for the swells when we get out past the breakwater," warned Grace's father. "She'll heel over a little. Look out, here it comes." He took the tiller from Grace and came about once more with seamanlike skill as the little boat tossed on its first true wave, lifting and falling with the great swell that came rolling to meet it from the other side of the Atlantic Ocean.

"Oooooohhh," moaned Grace.

"Want to take the tiller again?"

"I guess so." Grace reached out a trembling hand, faltered, and then clapped it against her mouth. She was going to be sick again. She leaned over the side and abandoned herself to misery.

"To loo'ard, Grace, for God's sake!" shouted her father. "Always throw up to loo'ard!"

"Sorry," sobbed Grace, rolling to the other side of the boat as it plunged into the hollow of the next wave. "Oooooohhh, stop, make it stop." It was just like a rollercoaster Grace had been on once at Revere Beach. That had been the worst moment in her life until now. She would never have guessed that going to sea would be like a ride on a rollercoaster. "Oooooohhh," whimpered Grace. "Stop! Please stop!"

"We'd better go back," murmured Mr. Jones, and as quickly as he could he turned the catboat around and headed back inside the breakwater. But he wasn't quick enough for Grace, who was stretched out flat on the bottom of the boat, sea and sky reeling around her, her stomach in a state of total convulsion.

"It's just the excitement and the heat. You'll be all right next week," said her father, weaving the little boat in and out among the moorings in the quiet water of the harbor. And then he told Grace some funny stories about famous sailors who had been seasick at crucial moments in history. Lord Nelson at Trafalgar, Admiral Dewey at Manila Bay. "Why did he say, 'You may fire when ready, Gridley'? Because he had to go below and throw up. That's a fact."

But Grace refused to be comforted. "Oh, Pop," she wept, "do you think I'll be seasick again next week?"

"No, no. It was just the excitement of the first time," said her father, half pushing, half pulling poor Grace out of the boat and up onto the dock, silencing with a hideous scowl the funny remark the boy on the dock was about to make.

But it was just the same the next Saturday morning. Grace's stomach was fine until the little boat slipped out of the breakwater and into the open sea. Then she was a goner.

"Was she sick again?" said Will, raising his eyebrows with surprise as Grace staggered upstairs after the third and last Saturday morning on the rolling deck, the billowing main.

"She was even sick in the car," said her father. "I'm afraid she's a landlubber, poor thing, whether she likes it or not."

"Oh, the poor, poor dear," said Mrs. Jones.

She had been sick in the car! Not only in the boat but even in the car! And also, Grace soon discovered to her horror, in the branches of her white pine tree. When she tried to climb it the next day she found herself clutching the trunk of the tree halfway up, overcome with vertigo, her eyes tightly shut against the sight of the horizon, which was dipping and righting itself and then dipping sickeningly once again.

"Galoot!" she muttered to herself scornfully in Captain Nancy language. "Donkey! Booby! Idiot! *Ooooooohhh!* Forgive me, Tom, forgive me—" Descending feebly from one branch to the next, she fumbled her way down to the ground again. Trueblue Tom was sinking fast. His health was failing. He was lying in his seaman's hammock, swinging dreadfully from side to side, uttering his last words. "Don't bury me at sea," groaned Trueblue Tom.

Grace revived him, of course, and let him follow her around the corridors of the Winslow S. DeForest School. But he was only a shadow of his former self. He was on his beam ends. He was puzzled and perplexed, and didn't know which way to turn. The first mate of *The Flying Cloud* was a landlubber now. He had been a phony from the start. He would never go to sea again.

Chapter 22

TEENIE
HAS THE
LAST WORD

While Grace was making the horrifying discovery that her wretched stomach was less seaworthy than the rest of her, her brother Will was coming closer and closer to a critical day of his own. He was getting ready to take the examination in Philadelphia for his ham radio license. If he passed the exam, if he could show that he was able to send and receive Morse code at the rate of ten words a minute, if he could draw the circuit of a Hartley oscillator, and if he knew the answers to a lot of other technical questions, then he would be licensed as a regular shortwave operator, with his own personal call letters, and he would be able to talk to other shortwave operators all over the world. If he passed the test Will was going to build a big antenna on top of the house, right on top of the tower room. But now he

154

was spending all his free time trying to increase his speed in sending and receiving. He was down-cellar all hours of the night, crouched over his set with his earphones clamped to his head. He ate all his meals there. He never seemed to do any homework. He grew pale from lack of sun. He had no time for anything but practicing Morse code. And for the first time in months he didn't seem to have any time to spare for Teenie Moon.

"Will Jones," Teenie would shout, stumping down the cellar steps, standing right beside his chair, hollering into his earphones, "you take that stupid thing off your head. I want to talk to you."

"Grumpf," Will would say, his eyes focused inward, his ears tuned only to the thin threadlike sound streaming out of his earphones. The threadlike sound was Morse code, of course, but it was also words, a succession of real words, flowing from some real person over there across the river in New Jersey, who was saying something important to another real person in Pennsylvania. And now the listener in Pennsylvania was responding. Sender and receiver were talking in Morse code at just a little too fast a clip for Will—they must be sending at the rate of fifteen to twenty words a minute—but every now and then he could catch a word or two. And with a twist of the dial he could bring in other delicate voices, from as far away as Florida and Ohio and Massachusetts. If he had, say, a tuned Zepp

155

antenna forty feet high, he would be able to get every state in the union, and even Europe and South America and Africa. The world was there, right there under Will's fingertips, waiting for him. He just had to get a little better at sending and receiving, just a little bit faster. There—what was that? Someone was calling "CQ! CQ!" Someone who wanted to talk to anybody who was listening! That was what CQ meant: is anybody listening? If Will only had his license he could pipe right up in reply and the two of them would have a friendly conversation. Then they would send each other their cards with their call letters printed on them, and Will would start a collection on his wall. Tokyo, Berlin, Honolulu! Before long he would have cards from all over the world on his wall.

But Teenie never took this kind of neglect lying down. Whenever she went down into Will's corner of the cellar and found him so engrossed and far-away, she would punch him and kick him and try to tip him out of his chair. And at last, in desperation, Will would wrench off his earphones, and pretty soon Teenie would have him laughing. She *was* funny, there was no denying it.

"Does that child still play with teddy bears?" said Mrs. Jones in disbelief, watching Teenie emerge from the cellar one day and go out the back door with a teddy bear under each arm.

"She says she's going to carry them up the aisle

when she gets married," laughed Grace. "Poncho's going to be her best man."

"You know who Teenie wants to marry, don't you?" said Sophie. "Will. She told me she's going to marry Will."

"Why, Will would never marry that funny little girl," said Mrs. Jones, scandalized by this piece of news.

"Don't be too sure," said Grace gloomily. She was scandalized herself.

But the romance, or whatever it was, was almost over, as it turned out. It came to a tumultuous end the very next day, after school.

Grace was lugging her books past the Moons' house, when Teenie leaned over the railing of the front porch and shouted at her, "Grace Jones! Tell that brother of yours I'm coming over!"

"Okay," said Grace. "Thanks for the warning."

"Wait! Grace Jones! Stop! Back up!"

"Why should I?"

"No, really, I mean it. Back up a few steps. Now walk forward again. There, I knew it! What's happened to you, Grace Jones? Where's that old stride?"

"What stride?" said Grace guiltily, looking down at her feet.

"You don't go *wham-wham* anymore. You know how you walk now? You walk like a *girl*. Oh, shame, shame, sailor-boy."

Grace flushed, took a giant leap over a puddle,

and then stalked down the path past the grapevine, stretching her legs with each step. But she seemed to have lost the knack. It was an effort. She had to really try.

"Don't forget! Tell your brother I'll be right over!"

So Grace told him. "Oh, Will," she warbled sweetly, poking her head through the cellar door, "your girlfriend's coming over to see you."

Will was soldering a tricky connection. He looked up with a blank face. "Oh, no, not again," he said.

"But I thought you liked it," said Grace evilly, studying Will's face.

"I just want to be let alone," said Will. And then he jumped out of his chair and leaped up the cellar steps three at a time, just as Teenie came running in the kitchen door.

"Hey, Will!" cried Teenie. But Will promptly disappeared down the narrow back hall and began thundering up the front stairs. "Will Jones, you wait for me!" Teenie lunged after him, but by the time she had reached the landing she could hear the battering thump of Will's feet on the way up to the room in the tower. So Teenie scuttled up those stairs too, screaming, "I'LL GET YOU FOR THIS, WILL JONES." Halfway up she stopped and stared at the door in the wall that opened on the attic tubroom. It was more like the door of a cupboard than the door of a room, but it was slightly ajar.

All was silence. Teenie stuck her head in the

door and looked around. Will was nowhere to be seen. But Teenie was sure he was in there. "I've got you now. You can't get away from me. I'll show you, Will Jones." She crawled into the narrow space beside the giant tub, and then she went bumping around on her knees in the attic-space, searching for Will among the boxes and suitcases and trunks, struggling over and around obstacles. She was just pouncing over the last of the huge trunks when she heard a new sound, a great splashing and sloshing, and, turning in horror, she saw Will. He was climbing out of the huge wooden tub, gasping for air, streaming with water, struggling for breath, laughing at the same time. Soaking wet, Will floundered over the edge of the tub, sprawled out the door and disappeared, while Teenie hurled herself over the trunks and suitcases and boxes again and dropped out of the tub-room onto the stairs that led to the room in the tower.

There was only one way he could have gone. The trail of wet footprints led straight up. From the tower room there was no escape. This time she had him for sure. He was trapped. "I'VE GOT YOU NOW, WILL JONES," squealed Teenie. Puffing and gasping, she threw herself up the last half of the staircase and emerged into the sunny silent room at the top of the house.

Will was nowhere in sight. The room was empty. Dismayed, enraged, Teenie ran around the room looking out the windows. Unless Will had sprouted wings and flown out the window over the Delaware River, he must have just vanished into thin air. Teenie stamped downstairs and found Grace and demanded to know where Grace's brother was hiding.

"Search me," said Grace, shrugging her shoulders.

Then Teenie burst into tears. She threw herself at Grace and wrapped her skinny arms around Grace's neck and sobbed. Grace patted her on the back, astonished. It was the only time she had ever seen Teenie Moon the least little bit out of sorts.

"Good-bye, Will Jones," wept Teenie, letting go of Grace and running out the door. "Good-bye forever."

But where *was* Will? Grace couldn't understand it either. She climbed the stairs to the tower room and looked around. He couldn't have just *disappeared*.

"Here I am," said Will. There he was, climbing in a window, grinning at Grace, soaking wet, filthy dirty. There was green mold from the shingles of the roof all over his wet clothes. "I climbed up on the top of the house," he said, "and just hung on by my fingernails."

"You didn't!" Grace was horrified. "You might have fallen and broken your neck." She laughed, and went back downstairs, feeling oddly contented. Her noble brother had regained his dignity at last.

But Teenie had her revenge on the Jones family. That same afternoon, as Grace was sitting in her corner on the back porch working on her scrapbook about the war in Europe, she suddenly became aware of an absence around her neck. Her locket! It was gone! Her precious eternal everlasting gold locket! *Teenie* had taken it. Teenie had taken it right off Grace's neck while she was crying about Will.

Furious, Grace burst out of the house, raced down into the hollow and up into the sunshine, stumbled and tripped over the grapevine, and galloped across the dirt road to the Moons' front porch. But just as she was leaping up the porch steps, something rattled on the wooden floor and skidded down the steps onto the cement walk. It was Grace's locket. And there was Teenie, peeking out the door, her eyes alight, her tear-streaked face glowing with a jolly smile. "Tell me, Grace Jones," she said gaily, laughter welling up in every word, "who do you think is better looking? Clark Gable or Mr. Chester? Which one, Grace Jones? Mr. Chester, I'll bet. Right? *Mr. Chester! Mr. Chester!*"

Chapter 23

MR. CHESTER
TIPS
THE SCALES

And Teenie wasn't finished yet. Next day in school she found Mr. Chester in the teachers' room with Miss Humminger, and she told on Grace.

"I know somebody who's sweet on you, Mr. Chester," confided Teenie, leaning in from the hall.

"They're all sweet on me," said Mr. Chester grandly, beaming at Miss Humminger, who tittered and blushed.

"Grace Jones, that's who it is," said Teenie. "She has your picture in a locket around her neck. She's just crazy about you, Mr. Chester." Then Teenie ran away.

"That dreadful tomboy," laughed Miss Humminger. "That girl is really insane."

"Oh, I don't know about that," said Mr. Chester.

162

"If I do say so myself, I think she has rather good taste in men."

"Well, I think she ought to be psychoanalyzed. Abnormality like that is upsetting to the other girls. It is upsetting to me personally. I look around my classroom at all those nice normal girls and boys, and then, *wham*! there's that *odd* child staring back at me. It spoils my day. She is denying her female role. I'll bet she has some kind of Oedipus complex, or something."

"Oh, no, Adelaide. I'm sure you're wrong about that. Quite, quite wrong. I'll tell you what *I* think. It's her whole basic fundamental *Weltanschauung*, her philosophy of life. That's what makes her a tomboy, in my humble opinion—a kind of divine discontent, a search for some sort of sublimity in the midst of her paltry bleak little life, a sacred dissatisfaction with things as they are, a kind of lofty yearning for a mystic harmony with the music of the spheres. It's quite marvelous, really."

"What about Chatty Peak?" giggled Miss Humminger. "Is she looking for the music of the spheres too?"

"Chatty Peak isn't a tomboy," laughed Mr. Chester. "Chatty Peak really *is* a boy."

"Whoops, there's the bell," said Miss Humminger, stubbing out her cigarette, clattering her coffee cup into the sink.

"Time for my little tomboy to come to orchestra practice," said Mr. Chester, with kingly good humor. "I think I'll give the child a big thrill." He finished his cigarette lazily, ambled off to the auditorium, strolled down the aisle to the orchestra pit, stepped onto the podium, rapped on the music stand with his baton, and glared around at the orchestra, getting exactly what he wanted, instantaneous silence. Then Mr. Chester smiled, to show that he was a good fellow after all, and began explaining the music they were about to run through for the first time, Smetana's tone poem about the River Moldau. The orchestra was going to perform it at the awards assembly on the last day of school.

"The flutes here at the beginning are just a pretty little babbling brook," said Mr. Chester, leaning over the twin girls who were the orchestra's flute section, Dolores and Dorothy Murphy, his less-than-an-eighth-of-an-inch of fat less than eight inches away from their twin faces. "Tiddily-tiddily, tiddily-tiddily, tiddily-tiddily-tiddle. Do you see, flutes?"

Nearly fainting with rapture, the Murphy twins lifted their flutes and blew into them. *"Whiff-puffety-whiff,"* they huffed, their lips pursed, their eyes crossed because Mr. Chester was standing so close. *"Whiff-whiffety-whiff."*

"That's the ticket. All right, cellos, you're next. The River Moldau has become a mighty torrent. The little rippling mountain stream is now the surging flowing river. Ba-BA, ba-BA, ba-BA, BA, BA, BA, BA!" The cellists, Loretta Twining and Gloria Dew, gazed up at Mr. Chester, their jaws hanging slack, their fingers turning to putty, their bow-arms limp with adoration. "Let's just run through it once, shall we?" said Mr. Chester.

"*Squee-scrape, squee-scrape, squee-scrape, scrape, scrape, scrape, scrape,*" wheezed the cellos hoarsely.

"Now for the bass viol," said Mr. Chester. He turned around and then stopped short. The big viol was still lying on its side. "Where's Donald Waldorf?"

"Coming," shouted Donald, racing down the aisle in the direction of the orchestra pit.

He was five minutes late. Mr. Chester stood stock-still. Everybody knew that Mr. Chester believed in absolute discipline, so they all stared in horror at Donald, who was obviously going to get it this time, as he blundered through a forest of music stands and chairs, snatched up the giant instrument and stood ready to go *zoom-zoom* at Mr. Chester's slightest command. But Mr. Chester's eye was skewering Donald to the wall. Mr. Chester didn't raise his voice. He merely lifted one arm, pointed with one finger at the door, and said one word: "*Go.*" Poor Donald put his bass viol down, shambled through the chairs and music stands again and made his way out of the auditorium.

Click-click! Mr. Chester's baton rapped sternly on

his music stand. "The beginning, if you please," he said. Then he raised his arms high and wide and looked fiercely left and right. The violinists and cellists and flutists and clarinet-players and horn-players and percussionists all looked at him obediently and prepared to saw, puff, toot and sock their instruments at the downward stroke of his baton.

But then Mr. Chester put his arms down again. Someone else was entering the auditorium and ducking into place at the piano.

It was Grace. She had been handing out towels in the girls' shower-room, and her successor, Martha Manning, had not arrived on time, so Grace had had to stay. The rule in the Girls Leader Corps was duty first and foremost to the Girls Leader Corps.

Grace sat at the piano with her wet hair plastered down, her steam-wrinkled fingers fumbling with her music, unaware that Mr. Chester was staring at her with his mouth open, and that the entire orchestra was looking eagerly back and forth between her and Mr. Chester to see what dire form of wrath he would wreak upon this latest miserable offender.

But Mr. Chester was an absolute monarch, and he ruled according to whim. He stepped off his podium and brushed through the violins and violas until he stood beside the piano. Grace, looking up, discovered that she was the sole object of his attention and of everyone else's too, and she started with surprise.

166

But Mr. Chester merely leaned on the piano and gave her one of his famous looks. "Good morning, Grace Jones," he said, his voice deep and thrilling.

"Good—good morning, Mr. Chester," stuttered Grace.

Mr. Chester beamed at Grace affectionately for a moment, and then he reached out with one hand and patted her wet hair. "I wonder," he mused tenderly, "just what goes on in that funny little head of yours?" Then he strode back to his podium, picked up his baton, looked sternly left and right and with a powerful downstroke of his baton he shouted, "TA-DAH!"

Swig-thump, responded the orchestra. Grace struck a miscellaneous assortment of sharps and flats. She was one seething tumult within.

"Very good," beamed Mr. Chester.

"I see Loverboy's in a good mood again," murmured George Wilkes, the bassoonist, to Henry Tonjer, the trombone player.

Chapter 24

THE DEATH
OF
TRUEBLUE TOM

It was like the pebble that tips the avalanche. Mr. Chester's light touch on Grace's head was all that was needed to start the avalanche hurtling down upon her, burying forever poor Trueblue Tom and Captain Nancy and Captain John, sinking for all time that gallant ship *The Flying Cloud*.

Grace was in love with Mr. Chester. Not the way she had been before, the way a cat can look at a king. Now she had a real crush, just like every other girl in the school. As for Mr. Chester, he hardly ever spoke to Grace again except about the music. And whenever that happened she would flutter and blush, just like all the rest.

And after school she began spending hours in Dot Moon's bedroom, sitting at Dot's dressing table, experimenting with this and that. Dot was lavish with

168

her jars and powders and ointments. She was the soul of generosity in passing along her knowledge of the art. She gave Grace one of her eyelash curlers as a present.

"Go ahead," she said. "Take it. It's all yours."

"Gee, Dot, thanks," said Grace. "You'll have to show me how it works."

Dot showed her how to open it up wide and then clamp it down hard. She looked at Grace enviously in her little three-sided mirror. "Gosh, Grace, I wish I had your nose."

"My nose is all right," said Grace. "But I have a fat face. I do, you can't deny it. I have a fat, fat face."

"No, no," soothed Dot. "It's just pleasingly plump. Besides, I'll show you how you can get a skinnier look by making a lot of curls on top of your head. Just watch this." Dot plugged in her curling iron, and then she spent the next half hour patiently frizzing a whole set of cylindrical sausage curls on top of Grace's head.

"They'll jiggle," worried Grace. She shook her head from side to side, and the sausages all jiggled. "See?"

"Just you wait," said Dot. Carefully, one by one, she skewered every sausage with a bobby pin. "There. Now try it."

Grace shook her head again. Her sausage curls stayed stiff and rigid, gripping her scalp.

"Now for the powder and rouge," said Dot.

Grace's middy had disappeared. She had forgotten all about it. After its disastrous adventures at Rehoboth Beach, Mrs. Jones had washed it and dried it on a towel and bundled it off to the attic in mothballs when Grace wasn't looking. To her mother's surprise and pleasure Grace never asked for it, and so Trueblue Tom's romantic uniform remained hidden away in the attic, buried deep down in a trunk with other mementoes of Mr. and Mrs. Jones's early married life.

Little by little the new Grace Jones crept out of her cocoon. She appeared full-blown in public for the first time on the last Friday before the end of school, at the awards assembly.

The awards assembly! At last the rings for the Best All-around Boy and the Best All-around Girl were going to drop out of the clouds in which they had been hovering so long, and land on the fingers they belonged to, endowing two people with a radiance of gold forever.

Which two? Daniel Margolis? Milly Lee? Harold Farley? Charley Blake? Dot Moon? Henry Tonjer? Chatty Peak? *Grace Jones?* Nobody guessed Marjorie Zednick anymore, because Marjorie's parents had taken her out of school altogether. Marjorie was getting ready for her debut as a young violinist, and she just didn't have time for ordinary classes. Grace had been there in the gym when Marjorie had turned in her Leader Corps uniform to Miss Bodecker. Marjorie had wept.

On the way to school in the trolley on the morning of the awards assembly, Dot Moon was calmly confident. She knew who would get the girl's ring. "No, no, they won't give it to me," she said. "They'll give it to you, Grace. Look at your marks. And your being in the Leader Corps and the orchestra. That's the kind of thing that counts."

"But I'm not like that," protested Grace. She meant that she didn't have that ringlike quality of being gold. But just the same her heart was beating with hope as she sat down at the piano in the orchestra pit while the rest of the senior class filed onto the stage. Grace's hair was clamped into sausage curls, her eyelashes were wrenched upward like spiders' legs, and she was wearing a new angora sweater her mother had bought at a sale at Dixie Brothers Dry. (Grace was suffering agonies because of the new sweater. The loose bits of cheap angora fluff kept floating off the sweater and getting up her nose.)

When Mr. Chester clicked his baton on his music stand and lifted his arms and looked around the orchestra in preparation for the downbeat, he got a shock. He dropped his arms and stared at his favorite tomboy in surprise. What had happened to Captain Bligh? Now she looked just like all the rest. That divine spark, that flaunting tomboy style, that carefree union with the infinite—where had it all

gone? It was too bad. And why was she wrinkling her nose like a rabbit? She was an odd duck, that girl. She would probably always be an odd duck.

Mr. Chester clicked his baton on his music stand again, scowled furiously around at his little flock, and then launched the awards assembly with the opening bars of Smetana's tone poem about the River Moldau. The flutes tiddled prettily like a babbling brook, the cellos surged like the mighty river, and Henry Tonjer's trombone bellowed out the final tempestuous union of the raging torrent with the thundering depths of the sea. Mr. Chester beamed at Henry as Hilda Schultz's cymbals brought the tone poem to a clashing close, and Henry blushed with pleasure. Then Henry and Hilda and Donald Waldorf and Grace Jones all struggled out of the orchestra pit and climbed the steps to sit down on the stage with the rest of the senior class. It was time for Mr. Fitzhugh, the commander of American Legion Post 104, to present the gold rings to the Best All-around Girl and the Best All-around Boy.

Mr. Fitzhugh was not used to public speaking. He kept clearing his throat and saying, "Pardon me."

". . . for her qualities of leadership, good sportsmanship, study habits, character and personality," said Mr. Fitzhugh, "American Legion Post One Aught Four is pleased to award this twenty-four carat gold ring to *krrrrrrmmmmmm*, *krrrrrrmmmmmm*, pardon me."

The girls all sat bolt upright in stiff rows on their chairs, staring at Mr. Fitzhugh with glazed eyes, their hearts pounding. But Mr. Fitzhugh's nose was tickling from a far-flung piece of fluff that had detached itself from Grace's sweater. He blew his nose in his pocket handkerchief, cleared his throat again, said, "Pardon me" again, and pronounced the name of Grace Jones.

The audience clapped. Grace got up in a dream and walked forward to receive her prize. "Thank you," murmured Grace. Then she sat down again, smiling modestly, feeling waves of jealousy washing toward her from the other girls.

She had got it! She had won the ring! Lo, her name had led all the rest! On either side of her the stiff arms of the other girls were rigid with disappointment. "Why, they'll hate me now," Grace said to herself in surprise. "They'll all hate me."

Now Mr. Fitzhugh was getting ready to announce the name of the Best All-around Boy, and Grace glowed again secretly. How wonderful to be the Best All-around Girl if Daniel Margolis were the Best All-around Boy!

". . . character and personality. The Best All-around Boy is *krrrrrrmmmmmm*! *honk*! Pardon me. The Best All-around Boy is Donald Waldorf."

Donald Waldorf? The audience was too astonished to clap. Surely they had heard the name wrong? But all the girls and all the boys on the stage

174

were turning around to stare in amazement at the back row, where Donald Waldorf was lurching to his feet, purple with embarrassment, and blundering past the others to receive his ring.

Grace couldn't understand it. How *could* they? Donald Waldorf wasn't *anybody*. He was just a *nobody*. Then with a flush of dismay Grace caught on. She understood. Dean Alexander must have voted against Daniel Margolis, her heart bursting, because he didn't do his Latin homework, and the other teachers must have voted against Harold Farley and all the rest because they were always cutting up in class. And probably they had voted against Milly Lee because she just barely got passing marks. And Chatty Peak was always getting into trouble with the teachers because she was so high-handed about missing classes to help Miss Bodecker in the gym. It wasn't the golden ones who got the rings, after all. It was the quiet ones, the ones who didn't ever do anything or say anything or *be* anything exciting. And as Grace discovered this wretched truth about the ring she had just won, she could feel that all the others were understanding it too. Why, the ring was stupid. It wasn't important after all. It just didn't matter.

Well, at least the others wouldn't hate her now for winning it, thought Grace unhappily. But they wouldn't like her for it either. The ring just didn't make any difference one way or the other.

175

They congratulated her, afterward, when the awards assembly was dismissed. The other members of the class were good sports. They shook Grace's hand and clapped Donald Waldorf on the back. Donald, pale and speechless, just stood there as if he had been hit on the head and was about to topple over. Grace got through the congratulations as quickly as she could and hurried away to her locker to get her books. She wanted to be by herself for a little while.

"Well, well, well. If it isn't the Best All-around Girl in person."

There was someone standing beside her locker, waiting for her. Grace's jaw dropped.

It was Chatty Peak. Or rather it was a girl who looked a little like Chatty Peak. She had Chatty's face, and she was standing in Chatty's old lazy athletic slouch, and one of her hands was resting on her hip with the fingers spraddled forward and the thumb splayed back, just the way Chatty's always did.

But she was wearing a dress. She was wearing a drab dreary droopy drink-of-water dress, a straightaway ordinary everyday dress. Grace had a couple of dresses just like it in her closet at home.

"Hello, there," said Grace, her voice faint with surprise.

Chatty was shaking her head from side to side, as if she were overcome with wonder and admiration.

176

"Grace Jones and Donald Waldorf, the Best All-around Girl and Boy in the whole class. Wow. Here's a present for you, Best All-around Girl." Then Chatty threw something at Grace as hard as she could, something she had been holding behind her back. It was a wet, dirty towel from the girls' shower-room. It hit Grace on the mouth with a soggy *SPLATTTTT!* and fell on the floor. "Just toss it in the laundry for me, will you?" snickered Chatty, turning away.

Grace was thunderstruck. Chatty had wanted to be the Best All-around Girl herself. Chatty was jealous. Chatty was mean. Grace picked up the wet towel and hurled it back at Chatty. "Toss it yourself," she said. By some miracle her aim was perfect. The wet towel *smacked* around Chatty's neck, *slapped* around both sides of her face, *thwacked* her sloppily on both cheeks, and then *flopped* around her shoulders like a dripping disgusting scarf.

Chatty stopped in her tracks, grunted with shock, turned right around, and yanked off the towel. Then she did something odd. She fumbled and fumbled at the neck of her dress. Her whistle, guessed Grace— she was fumbling for her whistle. She wanted to blow a piercing blast on her shining silver whistle. But the whistle wasn't there. Her uniform wasn't there. Her basketball shoes with the big rubber cleats that lifted her an inch off the ground, they weren't there either. Chatty stopped fumbling for her whistle, cleared her throat, and announced that she was going to tell Miss Bodecker about this, she was going to tell her right away, she really was. Then she picked up the soggy towel from the floor and drifted away, dragging the towel, leaving a wet trail behind her like a large snail. Her drab, dreary dress did not swirl and toss behind her like a Scotsman's kilt. It merely drooped and draped. She was gone.

"Bravo," said someone. "*Sic semper tyrannis.* Down with the tyrant."

Grace looked around again. This time it was Mr. Chester. He was clapping his hands with crisp smacks of his pink palms, making bright musical sounds that echoed and re-echoed from the metal lockers and the glazed tiles on the walls. He had seen the whole thing. He walked up to Grace, swept up her hand, kissed it, flashed her his brilliant smile, and strode away. (Mr. Chester was relieved to discover that his favorite tomboy had not lost her vital spark after all.)

Grace staggered off in the other direction, heading vaguely for her first class. She was flabbergasted. Part of her was disappointed because winning the ring wasn't all it had been cracked up to be, part of her was dumbfounded by the change in Chatty Peak, and part of her was delirious with joy because Mr. Chester had kissed her hand.

She kept looking at the hand that had known such a moment of glory. And of course every time she looked at the hand she saw the gold ring. There it was. THE ring. On *her* finger. She had won it. But she didn't deserve it. She wasn't gold, and she knew it, any more than Donald Waldorf was gold, any more than the DeForest girls had turned out to be fairy princesses. But then Chatty Peak wasn't gold either. Maybe nobody was gold like that. Grace stopped cold at the door of her classroom, put her books down on the floor, pulled the ring off her finger, put it back in its blue velvet box, and stuffed the box into her pocket.

At lunchtime Dot was waiting for her, and they stood in the cafeteria line together. "I told you so, Grace," said Dot. "Didn't I tell you you would win the ring? I'll bet you're happy now." There was just the faintest edge to Dot's voice. Grace knew what that meant. Dot thought the ring was something Grace really cared about. It was her kind of thing. "Let me see it," said Dot, reaching for Grace's hand. "Where is it? Aren't you going to wear it?"

"No," said Grace.

"Oh," said Dot. Then she nodded her head and grinned. She understood. She understood the whole thing.

Grace put a tuna-fish sandwich and a Dixie cup of ice cream on her tray. Then she reached into her pocket for her coin purse. "Whoops," said Grace, "I forgot my lunch money."

"Be my guest," said Dot, holding up her pocketbook.

"I'll pay you back," said Grace. The two girls carried their trays to an empty table in the corner and sat down side by side. And then Grace told Dot how she felt about Mr. Chester. Dot whistled, and promised not to tell. (Of course the news was no surprise to Dot, because Teenie had shown her Mr. Chester's picture in Grace's locket. But she pretended to be hearing about it for the first time.)

Talking *about* Mr. Chester was almost as thrilling as talking *to* him. Dot listened patiently as Grace went on and on, and nodded her head wisely and said what *she* thought and then listened some more. By the time the lunch hour was over, Dot and Grace were whispering and giggling in high spirits, and comparing the pictures of movie stars on the lids of their Dixie cups.

Chapter 25

MOVE OVER, SAMUEL TAYLOR COLERIDGE!

And then when she got home from school that afternoon, Grace discovered that she was the Best All-around Girl all over again. Her mother and father were waiting for her in the kitchen. Her father had come home especially to congratulate her. Her parents, it turned out, had known all about it for weeks. "Let's see it, Grace," said her mother proudly.

Grace opened the little blue velvet box and displayed the gold ring.

"Lo," said her father, clapping her on the back, "Grace Jones's name led all the—"

"Oh, please, *please*," groaned Grace, "don't say it."

"Aren't you going to put it on?" said her mother.

"No."

"Not ever?"

"I'm just going to put it away for now," said Grace. She went upstairs, stuck the box with the ring in it in a dresser drawer, and then jerked off her angora sweater because it was driving her crazy. She put on a clean blouse, and made her way downstairs to the back porch and her kitchen-cabinet desk.

Her father parted the curtain in the kitchen window and looked out at Grace. "What on earth has happened to that girl?" he said, shaking his head. "What's she doing to her hair, anyway?"

"She's stopped being a tomboy, I think," said Grace's mother. "Thank goodness."

"Well, I suppose it had to happen sometime. But I'm going to miss that fine careless rapture."

Grace's mother laughed. "Don't forget what you said before. The way she throws herself into things and goes overboard. She'll still do that, I'll bet."

"That's right. I guess the careless rapture is more or less built into that girl."

"And you know she couldn't go on climbing trees and wearing your old Navy uniform all her life. She had to stop sometime."

"Well, all I'm saying is I'm going to miss it, that's all."

In the meantime Grace was hard at work at her

desk on something new. She was beginning a new scrapbook on the subject of movie stars. She had started saving the Dixie cup tops from the cafeteria, and already she had a small collection. They were still a little chocolatey around the edges, although she had washed them as clean as she could. She brushed paste on the backs of them now—Claudette Colbert and Ginger Rogers and Gary Cooper and Jimmy Stewart and Clark Gable and Vivian Leigh and Leslie Howard—and stuck them into the scrapbook, four to a page.

Her father came out on his way back to work. "Is that your war news scrapbook, Grace?" he said.

"No, this one is about movie stars," said Grace.

"Oh. Well, so long. And congratulations again."

I'll be what I want, thought Grace stubbornly. I will make myself.

Then she put her movie stars away and reached into the cupboard over her head for something she hadn't looked at for a long time, her fragment of poetry about God and the universe. Putting the sheet of paper on the porcelain counter she read the solitary stanza over again. It was just as beautiful, just as miraculous as ever. Why couldn't she write any more of it? Had it been just a fluke, just a mistake, just an accident that would never happen again? Then suddenly Grace got another idea, and she picked up her pencil and began to write.

I will mould myself like clay,
I will hammer myself like stone,
And the hammer in my hand
Will be struck from my own breastbone.

My clay will be as soft
And pliable as grass—
But fired in the furnace
It will ring like glass.

They had come again, the rhymes. They had poured right through her onto the paper. Grace read them over and over, and they filled her with joy. She jumped up from her desk and ran down into the cellar to show her poem to Will.

But Will was too busy to pay much attention. He was going to take his radio operator's exam the next day, and he was in an agony of anxiety and anticipation. He glanced at Grace's poem, and then turned back to his radio.

"Listen," he said, holding his earphone away from his head so that Grace could hear the signal. "I can catch most of this. It's some guy in Georgia. Doesn't it sound awfully fast to you? I'll bet it's twenty words a minute."

"I'm sorry," said Grace. "I don't know if it sounds fast or not."

"I'll bet it is," said Will. He twiddled his dials nervously, testing himself over and over. The floor was awash with pieces of paper covered with circuit diagrams. Will was trembling on the edge of a new world.

Grace walked slowly back up the cellar stairs, reading her poem to herself once more. What, exactly, did it mean? She wasn't quite sure, although she knew it meant *something*. And where had it come from? Straight from Xanadu, thought Grace romantically. From Xanadu and Kubla Khan and the milk of paradise.

After all, she knew those old poems by heart. She couldn't unlearn them even if she wanted to. The hot and copper sky of the Ancient Mariner was still smoldering inside her head, and still echoing there too were the hollow and glittering chambers of Kubla Khan's caves of ice. It was the clashing together of the hot and cold—that was what did it. It was the huge empty spaces of the caverns and domes —that was where the new rhymes came from.

Grace took her poem back to her desk behind the piled-up newspapers and trash barrels and stuck it in her movie-star scrapbook for safe keeping, vowing to sit down and write a lot more whenever she got around to it. Then she stood looking down at the page of verse that had come out of her own head, and pride swelled within her.

"Move over, Samuel Taylor Coleridge!" cried Grace, sweeping her arms wide. Alas, the back porch wasn't big enough for vainglory, and Grace's right hand smacked into the kitchen cabinet and socked the flour bin with a jarring crash. The kitchen cabinet shuddered, and a little sprinkle of flour sifted down onto her poem like snow.

"Ouch, ouch," said Grace, sucking her sore knuckles. "That's what I get for bragging. I apologize to the universe. I apologize, I swear."

(*But beware of her, still. Beware.*)

Here are the two poems
by Samuel Taylor Coleridge
which Miss Humminger
assigned to Grace's English class.

Kubla Khan

In Xanadu did Kubla Khan
    A stately pleasure-dome decree:
Where Alph, the sacred river, ran
Through caverns measureless to man
    Down to a sunless sea.
So twice five miles of fertile ground
With walls and towers were girdled round:
And there were gardens bright with sinuous rills,
Where blossomed many an incense-bearing tree;
And here were forests ancient as the hills,
Enfolding sunny spots of greenery.

But oh! that deep romantic chasm which slanted
Down the green hill athwart a cedarn cover!
A savage place! as holy and enchanted
As e'er beneath a waning moon was haunted
By woman wailing for her demon-lover!
And from this chasm, with ceaseless turmoil seething,
As if this earth in fast thick pants were breathing,
A mighty fountain momently was forced:
Amid whose swift half-intermitted burst
Huge fragments vaulted like rebounding hail,
Or chaffy grain beneath the thresher's flail:
And 'mid these dancing rocks at once and ever
It flung up momently the sacred river.
Five miles meandering with a mazy motion

Through wood and dale the sacred river ran,
Then reached the caverns measureless to man,
And sank in tumult to a lifeless ocean:
And 'mid this tumult Kubla heard from far
Ancestral voices prophesying war!

The shadow of the dome of pleasure
Floated midway on the waves;
    Where was heard the mingled measure
    From the fountain and the caves.
It was a miracle of rare device,
A sunny pleasure-dome with caves of ice!

    A damsel with a dulcimer
    In a vision once I saw:
    It was an Abyssinian maid,
    And on her dulcimer she played,
    Singing of Mount Abora.
    Could I revive within me
    Her symphony and song,
    To such a deep delight 'twould win me,
That with music loud and long,
I would build that dome in air,
That sunny dome! those caves of ice!
    And all who heard should see them there,
    And all should cry, Beware! Beware!
His flashing eyes, his floating hair!
    Weave a circle round him thrice,
And close your eyes with holy dread,
For he on honey-dew hath fed,
    And drunk the milk of Paradise.

The Rime of the Ancient Mariner

PART I

It is an ancient Mariner,
And he stoppeth one of three.
"By thy long gray beard and glittering eye,
Now wherefore stopp'st thou me?

"The Bridegroom's doors are opened wide,
And I am next of kin;
The guests are met, the feast is set:
May'st hear the merry din."

He holds him with his skinny hand,
"There was a ship," quoth he.
"Hold off! unhand me, gray-beard loon!"
Eftsoons his hand dropped he.

He holds him with his glittering eye—
The Wedding-Guest stood still,
And listens like a three years' child:
The Mariner hath his will.

The Wedding-Guest sat on a stone:
He cannot choose but hear;
And thus spake on that ancient man,
The bright-eyed Mariner.

"The ship was cheered, the harbor cleared,
Merrily did we drop
Below the kirk, below the hill,
Below the lighthouse top.

"The Sun came up upon the left,
Out of the sea came he!
And he shone bright, and on the right
Went down into the sea.

"Higher and higher every day,
Till over the mast at noon—"
The Wedding-Guest here beat his breast,
For he heard the loud bassoon.

The bride hath paced into the hall,
Red as a rose is she;
Nodding their heads before her goes
The merry minstrelsy.

The Wedding-Guest he beat his breast,
Yet he cannot choose but hear;
And thus spake on that ancient man,
The bright-eyed Mariner.

"And now the Storm-blast came, and he
Was tyrannous and strong:
He struck with his o'ertaking wings,
And chased us south along.

"With sloping masts and dipping prow
As who pursued with yell and blow
Still treads the shadow of his foe,
And forward bends his head,
The ship drove fast, loud roared the blast,
And southward aye we fled.

"And now there came both mist and snow,
And it grew wondrous cold:
And ice, mast-high, came floating by,
As green as emerald.

"And through the drifts the snowy clifts
Did send a dismal sheen:
Nor shapes of men, nor beasts we ken—
The ice was all between.

"The ice was here, the ice was there,
The ice was all around:
It cracked and growled, and roared and howled,
Like noises in a swound!

"At length did cross an Albatross,
Through the fog it came;
As if it had been a Christian soul,
We hailed it in God's name.

"It ate the food it ne'er had eat,
And round and round it flew.
The ice did split with a thunder-fit;
The helmsman steered us through!

"And a good south wind sprung up behind;
The Albatross did follow,
And every day, for food or play,
Came to the mariners' hollo!

"In mist or cloud, on mast or shroud,
It perched for vespers nine;
Whiles all the night, through fog-smoke white,
Glimmered the white moonshine."

"God save thee, ancient Mariner,
From the fiends, that plague thee thus!—
Why look'st thou so?" "With my crossbow
I shot the Albatross.

PART II

"The Sun now rose upon the right:
Out of the sea came he,
Still hid in mist, and on the left
Went down into the sea.

"And the good south wind still blew behind,
But no sweet bird did follow,
Nor any day for food or play
Came to the mariners' hollo!

"And I had done a hellish thing,
And it would work 'em woe:
For all averred I had killed the bird
That made the breeze to blow.
Ah wretch! said they, the bird to slay,
That made the breeze to blow!

"Nor dim nor red, like God's own head,
The glorious Sun uprist:
Then all averred I had killed the bird
That brought the fog and mist.
'Twas right, said they, such birds to slay,
That bring the fog and mist.

"The fair breeze blew, the white foam flew,
The furrow followed free;
We were the first that ever burst
Into that silent sea.

"Down dropped the breeze, the sails dropped
     down,
'Twas sad as sad could be;
And we did speak only to break
The silence of the sea!

"All in a hot and copper sky,
The bloody Sun, at noon,
Right up above the mast did stand,
No bigger than the Moon.

"Day after day, day after day,
We stuck, nor breath nor motion;
As idle as a painted ship
Upon a painted ocean.

"Water, water, everywhere,
And all the boards did shrink;
Water, water, everywhere,
Nor any drop to drink.

"The very deep did rot: O Christ!
That ever this should be!
Yea, slimy things did crawl with legs
Upon the slimy sea.

"About, about, in reel and rout
The death-fires danced at night;
The water, like a witch's oils,
Burnt green, and blue, and white.

"And some in dreams assurèd were
Of the Spirit that plagued us so;
Nine fathom deep he had followed us
From the land of mist and snow.

"And every tongue, through utter drought,
Was withered at the root;
We could not speak, no more than if
We had been choked with soot.

"Ah! well-a-day! what evil looks
Had I from old and young!
Instead of the cross, the Albatross
About my neck was hung.

PART III

"There passed a weary time. Each throat
Was parched, and glazed each eye.
A weary time! a weary time!
How glazed each weary eye!
When looking westward, I beheld
A something in the sky.

"At first it seemed a little speck,
And then it seemed a mist;
It moved and moved, and took at last
A certain shape, I wist.

"A speck, a mist, a shape, I wist!
And still it neared and neared:
As if it dodged a water-sprite,
It plunged, and tacked, and veered.

"With throats unslaked, with black lips baked,
We could nor laugh nor wail;
Through utter drought all dumb we stood!
I bit my arm, I sucked the blood,
And cried, A sail! a sail!

"With throats unslaked, with black lips baked,
Agape they heard me call:
Gramercy! they for joy did grin,
And all at once their breath drew in,
As they were drinking all.

194

"See! see! (I cried) she tacks no more
Hither to work us weal—
Without a breeze, without a tide,
She steadies with upright keel!

"The western wave was all aflame,
The day was wellnigh done!
Almost upon the western wave
Rested the broad, bright Sun;
When that strange shape drove suddenly
Betwixt us and the Sun.

"And straight the Sun was flecked with bars
(Heaven's Mother send us grace!),
As if through a dungeon-grate he peered
With broad and burning face.

"Alas! (thought I, and my heart beat loud)
How fast she nears and nears!
Are those her sails that glance in the Sun,
Like restless gossameres?

"Are those her ribs through which the Sun
Did peer, as through a grate?
And is that Woman all her crew?
Is that a Death? and are there two?
Is Death that Woman's mate?

"Her lips were red, her looks were free,
Her locks were yellow as gold:
Her skin was as white as leprosy,
The Nightmare Life-in-Death was she,
Who thicks man's blood with cold.

"The naked hulk alongside came,
And the twain were casting dice;

'The game is done! I've won! I've won!'
Quoth she, and whistles thrice.

"The Sun's rim dips; the stars rush out
At one stride comes the dark;
With far-heard whisper, o'er the sea,
Off shot the specter-bark.

"We listened and looked sideways up!
Fear at my heart, as at a cup,
My life-blood seemed to sip!
The stars were dim, and thick the night,
The steersman's face by his lamp gleamed white;

From the sails the dew did drip—
Till clomb above the eastern bar
The hornèd Moon, with one bright star
Within the nether tip.

"One after one, by the star-dogged Moon,
Too quick for groan or sigh,
Each turned his face with a ghastly pang,
And cursed me with his eye.

"Four times fifty living men
(And I heard nor sigh nor groan),
With heavy thump, a lifeless lump,
They dropped down one by one.

"The souls did from their bodies fly—
They fled to bliss or woe!
And every soul, it passed me by
Like the whizz of my crossbow!"

PART IV

"I fear thee, ancient Mariner!
I fear thy skinny hand!

And thou art long, and lank, and brown,
As is the ribbed sea-sand.

"I fear thee and thy glittering eye,
And thy skinny hand so brown."—
"Fear not, fear not, thou Wedding-Guest!
This body dropped not down.

"Alone, alone, all, all alone,
Alone on a wide, wide sea!
And never a saint took pity on
My soul in agony.

"The many men, so beautiful!
And they all dead did lie:
And a thousand thousand slimy things
Lived on; and so did I.

"I looked upon the rotting sea,
And drew my eyes away;
I looked upon the rotting deck,
And there the dead men lay.

"I looked to heaven, and tried to pray;
But or ever a prayer had gushed,
A wicked whisper came, and made
My heart as dry as dust.

"I closed my lids, and kept them close,
And the balls like pulses beat:
For the sky and the sea, and the sea and the sky,
Lay like a load on my weary eye,
And the dead were at my feet.

"The cold sweat melted from their limbs,
Nor rot nor reek did they:

The look with which they looked on me
Had never passed away.

"An orphan's curse would drag to hell
A spirit from on high;
But oh! more horrible than that
Is the curse in a dead man's eye!
Seven days, seven nights, I saw that curse,
And yet I could not die.

"The moving Moon went up the sky,
And nowhere did abide;
Softly she was going up,
And a star or two beside—

"Her beams bemocked the sultry main,
Like April hoar-frost spread;
But where the ship's huge shadow lay,
The charmèd water burnt alway
A still and awful red.

"Beyond the shadow of the ship,
I watched the water-snakes:
They moved in tracks of shining white,
And when they reared, the elfish light
Fell off in hoary flakes.

"Within the shadow of the ship
I watched their rich attire:
Blue, glossy green, and velvet black,
They coiled and swam; and every track
Was a flash of golden fire.

"O happy living things! no tongue
Their beauty might declare:
A spring of love gushed from my heart,

And I blessed them unaware:
Sure my kind saint took pity on me,
And I blessed them unaware.

"The selfsame moment I could pray;
And from my neck so free
The Albatross fell off, and sank
Like lead into the sea.

PART V

"O sleep! it is a gentle thing,
Beloved from pole to pole!
To Mary Queen the praise be given!
She sent the gentle sleep from Heaven,
That slid into my soul.

"The silly buckets on the deck,
That had so long remained,
I dreamt that they were filled with dew;
And when I awoke, it rained.

"My lips were wet, my throat was cold,
My garments all were dank;
Sure I had drunken in my dreams,
And still my body drank.

"I moved, and could not feel my limbs:
I was so light—almost
I thought that I had died in sleep,
And was a blessèd ghost.

"And soon I heard a roaring wind:
It did not come anear;

But with its sound it shook the sails,
That were so thin and sere.

"The upper air burst into life;
And a hundred fire-flags sheen;
To and fro they were hurried about;
And to and fro, and in and out,
The wan stars danced between.

"And the coming wind did roar more loud,
And the sails did sigh like sedge;
And the rain poured down from one black cloud;
The Moon was at its edge.

"The thick black cloud was cleft, and still
The Moon was at its side;
Like waters shot from some high crag,
The lightning fell with never a jag,
A river steep and wide.

"The loud wind never reached the ship,
Yet now the ship moved on!
Beneath the lightning and the Moon
The dead men gave a groan.

"They groaned, they stirred, they all uprose,
Nor spake, nor moved their eyes;
It had been strange, even in a dream,
To have seen those dead men rise.

"The helmsman steered, the ship moved on;
Yet never a breeze up-blew;
The mariners all 'gan work the ropes,
Where they were wont to do;
They raised their limbs like lifeless tools—
We were a ghastly crew.

"The body of my brother's son
Stood by me, knee to knee:
The body and I pulled at one rope,
But he said naught to me."

"I fear thee, ancient Mariner!"
"Be calm, thou Wedding-Guest:
'Twas not those souls that fled in pain,
Which to their corpses came again,
But a troop of spirits blest:

"For when it dawned—they dropped their arms,
And clustered round the mast;
Sweet sounds rose slowly through their mouths,
And from their bodies passed.

"Around, around, flew each sweet sound,
Then darted to the Sun;
Slowly the sounds came back again,
Now mixed, now one by one.

"Sometimes a-dropping from the sky
I heard the skylark sing;
Sometimes all little birds that are,
How they seemed to fill the sea and air
With their sweet jargoning!

"And now 'twas like all instruments,
Now like a lonely flute;
And now it is an angel's song,
That makes the Heavens be mute.

"It ceased: yet still the sails made on
A pleasant noise till noon,
A noise like of a hidden brook
In the leafy month of June,

That to the sleeping woods all night
Singeth a quiet tune.

"Till noon we quietly sailed on,
Yet never a breeze did breathe:
Slowly and smoothly went the ship,
Moved onward from beneath.

"Under the keel nine fathom deep,
From the land of mist and snow,
The Spirit slid: and it was he
That made the ship to go.
The sails at noon left off their tune,
And the ship stood still also.

"The Sun, right up above the mast,
Had fixed her to the ocean:
But in a minute she 'gan stir,
With a short uneasy motion—
Backwards and forwards half her length
With a short uneasy motion.

"Then like a pawing horse let go,
She made a sudden bound:
It flung the blood into my head,
And I fell down in a swound.

"How long in that same fit I lay,
I have not to declare;
But ere my living life returned,
I heard, and in my soul discerned
Two voices in the air.

" 'Is it he?' quoth one, 'is this the man?
By Him who died on cross,

With his cruel bow he laid full low
The harmless Albatross.

" 'The Spirit who bideth by himself
In the land of mist and snow,
He loved the bird that loved the man
Who shot him with his bow.'

"The other was a softer voice,
As soft as honey-dew:
Quoth he, 'The man hath penance done,
And penance more will do.'

PART VI

First Voice:
" 'But tell me, tell me! speak again,
Thy soft response renewing—
What makes that ship drive on so fast?
What is the Ocean doing?'

Second Voice:
" 'Still as a slave before his lord,
The Ocean hath no blast;
His great bright eye most silently
Up to the Moon is cast—

" 'If he may know which way to go;
For she guides him smooth or grim.
See, brother, see! how graciously
She looketh down on him.'

First Voice:
" 'But why drives on that ship so fast,
Without or wave or wind?'

Second Voice:
" 'The air is cut away before,
And closes from behind.

" 'Fly brother, fly! more high, more high!
Or we shall be belated:
For slow and slow that ship will go;
When the Mariner's trance is abated.'

"I woke, and we were sailing on
As in a gentle weather:
'Twas night, calm night, the Moon was high;
The dead men stood together.

"All stood together on the deck,
For a charnel-dungeon fitter:
All fixed on me their stony eyes,
That in the Moon did glitter.

"The pang, the curse, with which they died,
Had never passed away:
I could not draw my eyes from theirs,
Nor turn them up to pray.

"And now this spell was snapped: once more
I viewed the ocean green,
And looked far forth, yet little saw
Of what had else been seen—

"Like one that on a lonesome road
Doth walk in fear and dread,
And having once turned round, walks on,
And turns no more his head;
Because he knows a frightful fiend
Doth close behind him tread.

"But soon there breathed a wind on me,
Nor sound nor motion made:
Its path was not upon the sea,
In ripple or in shade.

"It raised my hair, it fanned my cheek
Like a meadow-gale of spring—
It mingled strangely with my fears,
Yet it felt like a welcoming.

"Swiftly, swiftly flew the ship,
Yet she sailed softly too:
Sweetly, sweetly blew the breeze—
On me alone it blew.

"O dream of joy! is this indeed
The lighthouse top I see
Is this the hill? is this the kirk?
Is this mine own countree?

"We drifted o'er the harbor-bar,
And I with sobs did pray—
O let me be awake, my God!
Or let me sleep alway.

"The harbor-bay was clear as glass,
So smoothly it was strewn!
And on the bay the moonlight lay,
And the shadow of the Moon.

"The rock shone bright, the kirk no less,
That stands above the rock:
The moonlight steeped in silentness
The steady weathercock.

"And the bay was white with silent light
Till rising from the same,
Full many shapes, that shadows were,
In crimson colors came.

"A little distance from the prow
Those crimson shadows were;
I turned my eyes upon the deck—
O Christ! what saw I there!

"Each corse lay flat, lifeless and flat,
And, by the holy rood!
A man all light, a seraph-man,
On every corse there stood.

"This seraph-band, each waved his hand:
It was a heavenly sight!
They stood as signals to the land,
Each one a lovely light;

"This seraph-band, each waved his hand,
No voice did they impart—
No voice; but O, the silence sank
Like music on my heart.

"But soon I heard the dash of oars,
I heard the Pilot's cheer;
My head was turned perforce away,
And I saw a boat appear.

"The Pilot and the Pilot's boy,
I heard them coming fast:
Dear Lord in Heaven! it was a joy
The dead men could not blast.

206

"I saw a third—I heard his voice:
It is the Hermit good!
He singeth loud his godly hymns
That he makes in the wood.
He'll shrive my soul, he'll wash away
The Albatross's blood.

PART VII

"This Hermit good lives in that wood
Which slopes down to the sea.
How loudly his sweet voice he rears!
He loves to talk with marineres
That come from a far countree.

"He kneels at morn, and noon, and eve—
He hath a cushion plump:
It is the moss that wholly hides
The rotted old oak-stump.

"The skiff-boat neared: I heard them talk,
'Why, this is strange, I trow!
Where are those lights so many and fair,
That signal made but now?'

" 'Strange, by my faith!' the Hermit said—
'And they answered not our cheer!
The planks look warped! and see those sails,
How thin they are and sere!
I never saw aught like to them,
Unless perchance it were

" 'Brown skeletons of leaves that lag
My forest-brook along;
When the ivy-tod is heavy with snow,
And the owlet whoops to the wolf below,
That eats the she-wolf's young.'

" 'Dear Lord! it hath a fiendish look—
(The Pilot made reply)
I am a-feared.'—'Push on, push on!'
Said the Hermit cheerily.

"The boat came closer to the ship,
But I nor spake nor stirred;
The boat came close beneath the ship,
And straight a sound was heard.

"Under the water it rumbled on,
Still louder and more dread:
It reached the ship, it split the bay;
The ship went down like lead.

"Stunned by that loud and dreadful sound,
Which sky and ocean smote,
Like one that hath been seven days drowned
My body lay afloat;
But swift as dreams, myself I found
Within the Pilot's boat.

"Upon the whirl, where sank the ship,
The boat spun round and round;
And all was still, save that the hill
Was telling of the sound.

"I moved my lips—the Pilot shrieked
And fell down in a fit;
The holy Hermit raised his eyes,
And prayed where he did sit.

"I took the oars: the Pilot's boy,
Who now doth crazy go,
Laughed loud and long, and all the while

His eyes went to and fro.
'Ha! ha!' quoth he, 'full plain I see
The Devil knows how to row.'

"And now, all in my own countree,
I stood on the firm land!
The Hermit stepped forth from the boat,
And scarcely he could stand.

" 'O shrive me, shrive me, holy man!'
The Hermit crossed his brow.
'Say quick,' quoth he, 'I bid thee say—
What manner of man art thou?'

"Forthwith this frame of mine was wrenched
With a woeful agony,
Which forced me to begin my tale;
And then it left me free.

"Since then, at an uncertain hour,
That agony returns:
And till my ghastly tale is told,
This heart within me burns.

"I pass, like night, from land to land;
I have strange power of speech;
That moment that his face I see,
I know the man that must hear me:
To him my tale I teach.

"What loud uproar bursts from that door!
The wedding-guests are there:
But in the garden-bower the bride
And bride-maids singing are:
And hark, the little vesper bell,
Which biddeth me to prayer!

"O Wedding-Guest! this soul hath been
Alone on a wide, wide sea:
So lonely 'twas, that God Himself
Scarce seemèd there to be.

"O sweeter than the marriage-feast,
'Tis sweeter far to me,
To walk together to the kirk
With a goodly company!—

"To walk together to the kirk,
And all together pray,
While each to his great Father bends,
Old men, and babes, and loving friends,
And youths and maidens gay!

"Farewell, farewell! but this I tell
To thee, thou Wedding-Guest!
He prayeth well, who loveth well
Both man and bird and beast.

"He prayeth best, who loveth best
All things both great and small;
For the dear God, who loveth us,
He made and loveth all."

The Mariner, whose eye is bright,
Whose beard with age is hoar,
Is gone: and now the Wedding-Guest
Turned from the bridegroom's door.

He went like one that hath been stunned,
And is of sense forlorn:
A sadder and a wiser man
He rose the morrow morn.